BLUE TICKET

Sophie Mackintosh is the author of *The Water Cure*, which was longlisted for the Man Booker Prize in 2018 and won a Betty Trask Award in 2019. She also won the 2016 *White Review* Short-Story Prize and the 2016 Virago/ *Stylist* short-story competition, and has been published in *Granta* and *Tank* magazine, among others.

BLUE TICKET

Sophie Mackintosh

HAMISH HAMILTON
an imprint of
PENGUIN BOOKS

HAMISH HAMILTON

UK | USA | Canada | Ireland | Australia
India | New Zealand | South Africa

Hamish Hamilton is part of the Penguin Random House group of companies
whose addresses can be found at global.penguinrandomhouse.com.

| Penguin
Random House
UK

First published 2020

001

Set in 13.35/16.35 pt Fournier MT Std
Typeset by Jouve (UK), Milton Keynes
Printed and bound in Great Britain by Clays Ltd, Elcograf S.p.A.

A CIP catalogue record for this book is available from the British Library

HARDBACK ISBN: 978–0–241–40445–4
TRADE PAPERBACK ISBN: 978–0–241–40446–1

www.greenpenguin.co.uk

MIX
Paper from
responsible sources
FSC   FSC® C018179
www.fsc.org

Penguin Random House is committed to a
sustainable future for our business, our readers
and our planet. This book is made from Forest
Stewardship Council® certified paper.

For Ursula and Caerie

Fog-thick morning —
I see only
where I now walk. I carry
   my clarity
with me.

— Lorine Niedecker, 'Linnaeus in Lapland'

CONTENTS

Lottery

I

It began with the allocating of luck, our bodies pinballs inside a machine. It was the year of overlapping adolescences, when the girls started to faint and grow tall.

When I went to see my doctor at the clinic, the part of the wall where she measured our heights was dotted everywhere, as if with the eggs of flies. Mine was lost in there with the rest of them. Straighter, straighter, she said. Rapped my knuckles with a ruler. Look up! What do you see?

Just the dust gathering on the wallpaper of your ceiling, Doctor, I didn't say. She made notes on my body. I nibbled at the edges of my own skin. She wrapped sheets of gauze around my raw thumbs. Stop chewing on yourself, she said, and wrote down something which might have been *Failure to nurture*.

My father bought me a wiry grey dog when I turned eleven, for my heart. Run faster! I shouted at him when he couldn't keep up with me. This was love.

Cool light, spiders erupting from their silver webs inside my window frame. Out there, somewhere, was destiny. The dog and I were running towards it together. I liked to bury my face into his peppery fur, though I think I was allergic. It is possible that love was making me sick all along.

2

Drink a lot of milk if you want to speed it up, the knowing girls told us in the bathroom, between classes, as we massaged balm into our chapped lips. It hadn't happened to them yet but they had been able to find things out. Eat fats and oils, they said. We switched all the taps on and then we left for our lessons.

At dinner I took a spoonful of butter and ate it neatly. My father watched me and didn't say anything. I took another. Licked the spoon.

Be careful in your wanting was a slogan written on the wall of the clinic. I must have read it five hundred times over the course of that one year alone. My legs swinging back and forth on the orange plastic chair of the waiting room.

Girls left one by one throughout the term. No goodbye parties, no notes. By the time it was my turn, barely anybody remained. It was me and two other girls and the boys my age in the classroom, pushing our pencils across paper as we multiplied and subtracted and memorized underneath the sun's passage.

I felt no great fidelity to the concept of free will. At fourteen I had been awaiting the future for months. I sat for hours on the yellow tiles of my father's bathroom with my knees drawn up to my chest, as if I could compel my body onwards with the force of my thoughts. I couldn't rejoice in anything, except that each event brought me nearer to adulthood, the clear and shining horizon of it. It was as if we had to swim through mud to get there, an estuary barrier to us reaching the ocean. *Get through this*, I wrote on the back of my school notebook. Private mantra. I felt very advanced to have made such peace with myself. I knew nothing, obviously.

All of this I spoke about to Doctor J, a harried pale woman, owner of the marked wall. Our growing brains were stored on tapes in her filing cabinet, which held a psychic onslaught of numberless teenage girls waiting to be sifted.

What is your mind doing lately? she used to ask me, and I would say the same thing every time, which was It's not doing anything at all, which was also often the truth. I slept deeply and walked in the forest with my father's gun after school, looking for the shivering bodies of rabbits, though I never fired it when I was alone. I became sentimental about pine cones and poetry, and swam my prescribed laps at the leisure centre with the other girls my age, walking home along the grey country road bordered with greenery.

As the year drew on, long red marks welted my thighs, mysteriously. Skin stretching, the doctor said. You'll be tall. At the time I didn't believe her. On slow days, I prayed for my bleed to come. Prayed to nature to make it happen, to the wet grass and the sky. My mother's locket waited for me in my father's sock drawer. It wasn't locked away, but it was empty. My mother was buried in the grey cemetery outside of town. Her ticket might have been buried with her. I didn't ask.

My father took me to a restaurant. It was my first time playing at adulthood, and I didn't do a good job of it. Cracked, hollow bread rolls; I ate three of them very quickly. I saw the sad mushrooms in the carbonara as snails, and then could not eat those. Tender heart, my father called me then. He was a little angry. We had wine and I drank a splash big enough to coat the glass, but no more. It made my tongue feel lively. My father showed me how to swill the wine around and what the tidemarks told you. Like reading tea leaves, he said. I have looked into the wine and seen the future. It lives at the bottom of the bottle.

When all the wine was gone he lifted up the empty bottle and held it to his eye like a telescope. See? He laughed, but I did not ask what the future held.

She would have wanted you to pick a blue ticket, he said to me as we waited for the bill, but he did not elaborate. I did not want to seem stupid and ask, so instead I nodded. It was only trying to fall asleep, later on, that I realized what he had been telling me about my mother.

He was young to be a father. At the weekends, his friends came round to the house and drank beer and watched me. They played cards but not games that I recognized. One two, one two, they chanted as they threw the cards down. Another beer. I lay on my stomach in the dark in the hall, where they could not see me. I wanted to watch and not to be watched. It was fundamental to my desire. You do not understand that at fourteen. But I can understand it now.

In the cinema, later in the year, my fingertips slid around inside a bucket of popcorn. A boy sat next to me. I felt him put his hand out to me as if he were swimming. The hand moved up and down in the air until it reached my body. Hand found my shoulder, my chest. I let it rest there, peacefully. The film ended. The hand lifted. The boy left before I could look.

At school, the girls' bathroom was almost always empty, by then. Nobody left the taps running.

One day the grey dog became fat and even slower. It turned out she was a girl. She lay down and small blind things came out of her, pink and bleating, like hearts. My father did something with them. Set them into the wilderness, or gave them new homes. I chose to believe this.

It was the dog I thought about years later, when I looked down at my stomach, and there it was. Undeniable. I, too, would be slow. I, too, would lie down upon the ground. Cold ground. Blue morning.

You should have touched them, said the last girl at school apart from me. You would have been their mother. They would recognize your scent, and your scent only. A sad, streak-of-water girl, with unnerving pale eyes. I didn't like to think I was her sort, but here I was. Here we were. She placed a sandwich, carefully, inside her mouth. In my room at home I sniffed at my armpits, just to see. It seemed unidentifiable. It seemed like anyone else's stink. Nothing that anything would call home.

3

One day, finally, there was a red slick in my underwear. In the shower I washed my body with care, unfamiliar blood spooling thinly down my legs. A clot of dark jelly fell out of me. I felt, calmly, that perhaps I would die. Instead I put on the dress that had been hanging on my bedroom door for the past year; pink satin, sprigged with white flowers at the hem and neckline, a petticoat underneath that scratched at my knees. It smelled of the damp, of the accumulated sweetness of the cheap perfume that I sprayed dutifully on my body every day. I went and twirled in front of my father, who fetched the locket and gave it to me. Don't put it on yet, he said.

We got a taxi because it was a special occasion, although it was a long way; through the hulking shape of the nearest town, back out into the outskirts, past wooden houses like ours. The taxi driver had a plastic ice cream box with foil-wrapped chocolate hearts. Take two! he insisted, then put the box back under his seat.

Pretty girl, he said to my father, who said Watch it, smiling but not smiling, and then the two of them were silent for the rest of the journey. The hearts contained dark cherries. I folded both pieces of foil into one speck and pushed it into the gap between my seat and the door.

The lottery station was a lot like the clinic: two storeys of pale brick, a flat roof. When we pulled up, the emissary outside was smoking a cigarette, but he threw it into the road when he saw us. Congratulations, he said to me. He led us inside to where the others waited.

The floorboards were wooden, varnished aggressively. Countless feet had scuffed that floor. It pooled the reflections of all the lights – spotlights from the ceiling, a lamp on the desk where a man in a dark suit sat on an orange plastic chair, watching us, legs crossed. He could have been a doctor, but he wore no white coat, no white plastic gloves. There were four other girls in their own dresses sitting in a row on a wooden bench, flowers both real and fake pinned to chests. They were not the girls from my school. One wore velvet, two wore tulle, and the other wore satin like me. I took a shine to the girl in satin. Same species.

We lined up, waiting to pull our tickets from the machine, the way you would take your number at the butcher's counter. The music popular that year played from speakers on the ceiling. Just gravity enough. Just ceremony enough. Not necessarily such an important thing, after all.

My name was called first. They watched me as I walked the length of the room, towards the machine inside its cloaked box. I put my hand in it. I was apprehensive but ready for my life to be decided. I closed my eyes and thought about my father with the wine bottle to his eye. The machine was silent as it discharged a sliver of hard paper into my hand. It was a deep cobalt. Congratulations, the possible doctor in the dark suit said to me.

The other girls followed, each taking their own ticket from the machine in turn. Almost a full house! he exclaimed at the end, reading a piece of paper spat out from the machine. We huddled and compared tickets. They were all blue, except for one, which was white. The girl with the white ticket was escorted into a separate room by the doctor and another emissary. We watched the three of them walk through an unlit doorway. When the doctor came back he clapped his hands twice. You have been spared, he said with a terrible benevolence.

At the desk, the emissary who had been on the door wrote down the results, to communicate to homes, to clinics, to places distant and important that we did not know about. One by one we were called into another room, a different room to the girl who had pulled the white ticket. I lay on a reclining bed with a crisp paper cover, and another doctor, this one a woman and comforting, almost, in the familiar white coat, told me to fold up my knees. She pushed something inside me that hurt, a sharp and spidering pain. What is it? I asked, and she said, Your doctor will explain it all when you get to wherever you're going. She said *when* and not *if*, and I was grateful for that. Behind me I left a large rose of blood on the paper.

The bathroom of the lottery house was filled with yellow light, the veins of my thin neck standing out underneath it. I was a plucked chicken with badly applied eyeshadow, but the locket was around my throat now. There was a long, low mirror above the sink, a wicker chair in the corner and two bathroom stalls painted peach. In the mirror I watched the other girls leaning against the wall. Toes flexing. Eyes raised to the ceiling, moving to the door when the girl with the white ticket came in to join us, then back to the ceiling. There was a dying flower arrangement at the corner of the sink, gaps of oasis showing through pink carnations. The music came through in here too, speakers in the ceiling or underneath the sink.

At first I kept looking at the girl who had drawn the white ticket, the other girl in satin, though hers was pale blue and dirty at the hem where it dragged. Her eyes were red. I had the urge to take her arm and run with her somewhere, out to the woodland where I used to smoke with the other girls in my class between lessons, beyond the broken barbed wire of the school perimeter where the teachers could not see us. But I did not touch her; I made myself stop looking.

Inside the cubicle I spent some time reading the names and dates scratched on the door. With the safety pin that held on my fake peony corsage I engraved *Calla, Blue Ticket*, a smiley face and the date underneath. The swell of relief, smooth and natural as a muscle. I would never have children. And I was glad. I had been a child myself, not so long ago. I did not want to put any other puny creature through that.

I went with the rest of the girls back to the lottery room, where our parents stood lined up. There was a table with pots of tea and coffee, biscuits and thin sandwiches on china plates, packets of tissues. The doctor who had supervised the whole thing stood in front of the parents, as if we had interrupted them mid-address. Maybe we had. The mothers smiled. The fathers looked grim.

An emissary handed us each a bottle of water, a compass and a sandwich from the table, wrapped in a napkin. We did not get to pick the filling. The bottle given to the white-ticket girl was larger than ours, I noticed, and she received two sandwiches. It was happening immediately, the diverging of our paths, no time to spare.

Go, the doctor said to us. To the place of your choice. Walk into it. Anywhere but here. Congratulations.

I met my father's gaze. I had a city in mind. He looked back at me and nodded his head.

We walked out together into the cool night. The adults stayed in the light, for coffee and refreshments, to debrief with the doctor. We might see our parents again, we might not. Some of the girls halted at once when we got outside. They didn't know where to go. New and bewildered as the fawns I saw at the edges of the trees, in the dusk. The girl with the white ticket, though, she walked directly into the woods, the lights of our torches bouncing off the satin until she was gone into the dark. We were not so different.

I put the compass in the palm of my hand. North or south, east or west. The flicker of the needle, the splintered light of the moon on its glass casing. I knew I could do this; could prove myself something beyond chewed-up cuticles and the mould smell of the bathroom and boys in the dark, fumbling for something I was willing to give but barely had. My life was out there, ahead of me. I had to run to it, now that the shape was cast.

Some of the girls followed me as I set off down the pale stretch of road. I listened to the pad of their feet behind me, unwilling to let them come closer. One of the girls was crying for her mother, but her mother would not come. Nobody would come.

4

That's how your life becomes a set thing, written and unchangeable. It was an object that did not really belong to me, and to wish for any other was a fallacy at best, treasonous at worst.

Blue ticket: Don't underestimate the relief of a decision being taken away from you.

Blue ticket: I was not motherly. It had been judged that it wasn't for me by someone who knew better than I did.

Blue ticket: There was lack in my brain, my body, my soul, or something. There was a flaw I should not pass on. A warmth I was missing.

Blue ticket: My life was precious enough as it was. I wasn't to be risked.

Blue ticket: Some called it a noble sacrifice, others a mercy.

It meant a different thing every time I thought about it.

Years were frenetic, then calmer. They ticked with the inevitability of a metronome, some fallow and some interesting. Things could happen to a blue-ticket woman the way they might not for a white-ticket. Spirit of adventure. In practice, life felt smaller than that expansiveness promised. In the dark night I stood in my kitchen, smoking, watching the lights of my neighbours go off one at a time. I no longer asked men the age of my father to hit me in the face or stayed up for three nights at a time. I lived a mostly quiet life. My impulses were not always as uncontrollable as they seemed. By now I knew broadly which ones could make me happy, and which would not.

Sometimes I became aware that there was somewhere I could not go. And I wanted to go there. Who wouldn't, when told it was impossible? Motherhood was the last perversion; otherwise known as loving and being loved. It was the only one closed off to me.

I want. There was a purity to that feeling that other sensations lacked, a simplicity, even as it remained the most complicated thing in the world.

Sometimes I would still go out looking for trouble. Sometimes I would sit up at a bar on the other side of the city and order drink after drink, staring at someone until they stared back, and then the dance began — inelegant but replete with its own pull and push. These rituals felt important to me. They made an object of my desire, helped me to feel out its edges and crevices. And yet the shape of it slid away from me like water.

Choice is an illusion, said a woman redoing her lipstick next to me in the bathroom mirror of a bar one evening. Don't you ever think about how everything is just completely futile?

I hadn't actually said anything. I do even now have that sort of face where strangers often talk to me, ranting or confessing, like I am someone they already know. This woman was more beautiful than me. She had hair feathering around her jaw, a mouth painted the colour of dark blood. Maybe she was very drunk, or maybe she was an emissary, designed to show us what good blue-ticket women looked like and felt, how free one could be if one totally embraced what one was given. I wasn't sure if emissaries did operate like that, but I had my suspicions. I wanted to kiss her anyway, because I still believed in beauty, because I wanted her good attitude to infect me, because I was also drunk, because I was never satisfied.

I saw this sort of woman everywhere once I started to look. I had counted myself among their number, and then one day they seemed like secret agents out to seed the word of independence, of pleasure-seeking and fulfilment. Isn't this good, they said from beneath the canopies of nightclub smoking areas, from tables where they sat alone, from cars and train carriages and beds, some in elegant suits or other uniforms to show their importance. They made impressive things and spent their time on worthwhile pursuits and I had been one of them, and the togetherness had sometimes felt like being one of a flock of lovely birds pushing through the hot space of the sky, and it was good, that was the thing, it was really so good, but now there was something happening to me, and I found I had little control over it.

But what's wrong with being exploratory, I justified to myself. Just being intrepid in my wants. I had always wanted more, had believed that this was an intrinsically good thing, that even when you didn't know exactly where a want would take you, going along with it could be illuminating. Fun, at the least.

(Do you want to end up dead? I had been asked by my doctors over the years.

Not always, I said. Not usually.)

Some nights I dreamed I was caught in a dark room with no windows or doors, a room from which there was no way out, and there was a pain in the centre of my chest, below tissue and bone, a pain that was part of me, though I resented and feared it.

On the road all those years ago I had seen something I do not think I was supposed to see. The white-ticket girl in the back of a car driven by an emissary from the lottery building. She had rolled the window down, a sliver of her face pressed to the gap. She looked wild, but I do not think she was being stolen away. She was being protected. I considered waving the car down and asking if I could get in too. I wondered if I had missed some vital instruction, and I watched the sleek lines of the car as it went down the road, until it was no longer visible.

It wasn't fair. Sometimes I came out from the dreamed dark room with those words on my lips, as if I had been saying them over and over. It wasn't fair.

When I thought about burning my life to the ground, which I was thinking about increasingly often, I wondered whether there were white-ticket women who wanted to burn theirs to the ground too. To be alone and unbeholden to all, and to find the glory in it – because there was glory in it; I could still see that glory as if from a distance, like it was somewhere I had left, the light of it far from me now and unreachable.

In its place came desires so alien that I could only assume they had been inside me for a long time, like splinters or shrapnel waiting to be pushed to the surface. Desires I had never even encountered. Like: holding a soft thing with large eyes, or humming a song without words. In the supermarket I cradled a hemp bag of sugar, six pounds in weight, then put it back immediately.

I spent a lot of time thinking about the curling hands of infants, about hot milk. I thought of the idea of someone coming home to you every day, of the concept of need and being needed. I opened a bottle of red wine just like my father, and by the end I was reaching for my locket and looking at the unspoiled blue and thinking: *white ticket*. I was thinking that a mistake might have been made somewhere and actually the life I had stepped into was the wrong one. Road not taken, or rather a road closed off to me.

I could not tell Doctor A about any of this. I could not ask him who gets to decide, who had been behind the machine in the lottery station all those years ago, the cramps of that first bleed twisting my stomach up like a wet sock.

I could not ask anyone. It was between me and my desire: stringy as the rind of a bean, me and it alone at night, with the moon shining down, and the only path visible was one absolutely forbidden to me.

And yet I wanted it, wanted it, wanted it.

Home

I

Eighteen years after the lottery. I stood in the bathroom of my home, milk-pale, meeting my own gaze in the mirror without cringing. On the floor below the sink there was a bottle of vodka from the freezer, a tumbler, tweezers and a small pair of pliers. A wedge of lime on the edge of the glass. I wore only my underwear, a white cotton bra and knickers, stuck to me with sweat. I poured another drink, put a folded-up flannel in my mouth to bite on. Crouched my body over, put my hand tenderly inside myself, and braced. I was forever amazed at the places your mind could compel your body to go. It didn't feel strictly possible that they could act in such opposition, but then the proof was everywhere.

For weeks there had been a new and dark feeling inside me. A strange, ravaging ghost that gave me recurrent headaches at my temples, and even dosing up with the extra tinctures prescribed by Doctor A, three sweet spots on the vein under my tongue, did nothing. It was a kind of desire that hadn't felt so different from other desires at first, so I hadn't seen the harm in nurturing it. I was used to wants that were instinctual, but this went somehow beyond. I hadn't known I was capable of such hunger, or such grief. In the bathroom with my hand inside myself I knew that I was giving in to it, following it into the uncharted parts of myself. It was going to take me somewhere I could not come back from, and I welcomed it, a little afraid but mostly exhilarated, like I was about to plunge into open water.

My fingertips brushed wire and the meat of myself. There was a feeling of fundamental wrongness, like an electric shock, and I realized I needed the tweezers. Oh please oh please, I said silently, imploring something I didn't believe in. The flannel was slick with my spit. A third try, this time with the slender pliers I used mainly for small household jobs. A broken sink, a loose bolt. I was attending to myself. I was elsewhere. Inside me, something came loose and I tugged. My hand skidded. I pulled the wire out and it was so small, a wishbone. When I threw it on the floor it beaded blood against the white tiles. More vodka, poured from bottle to mouth, my stomach churning. Easy, easy, I said to my body, like it was a spooked horse. The worst is over now.

2

I had been seeing Doctor A for five years by that point. One day I had come in for my usual appointment to find him sitting on the reclining chair as if he had always been there. Nobody could tell me what had happened to my previous doctor. But Doctor A was my third one, and my favourite, if truth be told.

A doctor is a sort of mother, Doctor A told me during our first session, and I laughed because it was both absurd and true. That's the kind of patient I'm going to be, just so you know, I told him.

Doctor A listened well, but was not afraid to speak. Sometimes I wished he were more afraid to speak. It's good for you, he said. It's good for you to hear the things you don't want to hear. He filled vials with my blood for mysterious purposes and observed the fluctuations of my weight and blood pressure. He nodded and gave me prescriptions written on yellow paper that I sometimes filled and sometimes crumpled into a ball and pressed down in the bins of the clinic bathroom, underneath used tissues, depending on how I was feeling that day. Occasionally I asked for specific pills but he always refused and said, Nice try! If you wanted something you had to go the circuitous route. Inventing symptoms, trying to trick him.

Oh, you want the green ones, he would say, tapping his pen on his

23

notepad in a way that transfixed me. He had very beautiful hands, though I tried not to notice how beautiful they were. I didn't like to examine those kinds of feelings too much, but I was reminded when he came close to me or when he looked good that some women had sex with their doctors in order to obtain a positive report, or just because the transference was no longer resistible. Transference was seductive, I had to admit, though I had never slept with my doctor, and was proud of it.

Mostly, though, I did not think much about Doctor A. He was just part of my routine, like morning laps around the green in the centre of our houses, neatly cutting up the slower runners. The other women and I wore similar nylon shorts, our lockets hitting exactly where our ribs shielded our hearts. Hello, we said sometimes, but more often we were silent. We lived outside the heart of the city, bounded by looped roads. It had been hard to sleep because of the traffic when I first moved, but now I needed the sound of it, the windows open wide to the white noise.

Following each run I made the longish walk to the laboratory where I worked, my lab coat in a nylon rucksack. There was a comfort in knowing I was moving towards a place of total predictability. As I walked I smoked exactly two cigarettes and drank coffee from a white ceramic flask. My nails were bitten to the quick and I could not wear nail varnish due to my work. The further I got into the city the more people joined me, men and women walking ahead or behind, smoking their own cigarettes and drinking from their own flasks. I stopped outside the lab to stub the second cigarette out on to a stone wall and tie my hair back. Looped elastic once, twice. You don't have to go in, I started saying to myself, kindly, but of course I always went in.

3

On Fridays when all the work for the week was done, the dangerous chemicals locked up, our supervisors brought out dark bottles of wine. We drank it together out of thick plastic tumblers that marbled the light, sitting on the wiped-down benches and swinging our legs. It was my favourite part of the day, of the week. We had waited for it all through the afternoon. The wine was sustaining as a soup, dark and rich in our mouths, and I could feel it benefitting me from the first sip, setting the wheels in motion, sparking the wildness up or dampening it down.

We changed in the bathroom into our going-out clothes. My tights were laddered already. They were always laddered. The tiles of the bathroom were deep green edged with white, and the lights were weak. In our reflections, bouncing back at us from long mirror, from vast stainless-steel sink, we belonged to the night. The small window high up on the wall let in a sliver of the sky where it was a clear ultramarine, deepening.

Girlhood was gone. Girlhood was over and dead for us all. We didn't miss it. In its place, anything could happen. We envisioned parties studding the city, people we were destined to meet waiting for us in pools of streetlight, in the places we expected them least. If you were a blue-ticket your life could change at any time, you could make it change at any time, and we were alternately complacent and anxious about the possibilities contained within that freedom.

After doing our hair we helped each other with our makeup, shared a lipstick around like a cigarette and then shared real cigarettes around after that, walking to the bars, still passing a bottle of the wine from hand to hand. I tilted it to the sky and drank deeply. Some ran down my chin and I wiped it off with my fingers. I loved the ritual, the film of the alcohol on my lips, the hairspray smell, how we lifted up each other's hair to spritz perfume at the soft skin where the neck met the jaw. I even loved how sometimes I fell before we had reached the bars, kerb coming up to sky, and my friends rallied around to pull me back up, a skinned knee maybe, my shins permanently bruised. No judgement. Bringing me back up to where I should be.

There was a man in the third bar we went to, drinking beer from an unmarked glass. He was over a head taller than me and that was the first thing I noticed, and the second was his broad and slightly curved shoulders in black cloth, the shoulders of a kind person, as if he were aware of the space his large man's body took up, and while not apologetic for it, he did not walk unthinkingly through the world. *That will do*, I thought.

The other women fell away. He and I drank short, honey-coloured cocktails that sent out a halo of warmth in the darkness of the bar. His name was R and he was older, but not by too much. He paid for the cocktails with a flourish. A roll of notes kept in his back pocket, his shirt bleached white. It was hard not to touch him. Much later on, when we had moved to a table in a corner, and when we were drunk, very drunk, I showed him the blue ticket in my locket, but only for a second. Snapped it open then closed, like a hungry mouth. Some men would have been put off, but not him. He flipped a beer mat between his fingers. Good, he said. I prefer it that way.

I took a mouthful of the golden drink to stop me saying anything rash. He put his hand on my knee and left it there. Desire turned up in me with a kick, a skipped heartbeat. All of my colleagues had gone and I hadn't even noticed. Outside the bar he gathered me into a lightless corner and on to him. He kissed me hard on the mouth and I put my fingers through his belt loops and pulled him against me for a second, several seconds, before pushing him away, both my palms against his chest, then running to the train station over the street covered with rain, exultant, my body full of the dark feeling, not turning back, though I knew he would be looking.

The dark feeling by then was a shimmering, liquid thing, like a pool of blood or a black opal. It was a kind of raging joy, is how I can best explain it. I sobbed while I waited for my train, but I wasn't sad.

On the way home the train was too bright and there was one other person on it, a woman with red hair and a long skirt, two spots of colour high up on the bones of her face, who met my eyes dead on and then stood up and walked down the train carriage to sit elsewhere, and I thought perhaps it was my weakness that had repelled her, that she had sensed it inside me and she wanted no part of it. Or maybe we were just two drunk women on a train and she wanted to be left alone.

So I met my own eyes in the window instead, the sheer dark as we passed through a tunnel, and my face was pale and drawn, my hair was a mess, and when I got in I walked straight into my bedroom and lay down fully clothed, a thick taste in my mouth. And I knew very well what sort of woman I was, and I did not want to be that woman any more – not the sort you would move away from on the train, not the sort that would allow herself to be kissed by strangers, crudely, where the empty bottles from the night were set out in boxes – and I thought *Please*, I thought *Please, please, please*, like a charm, until sleep took me over.

4

Memories from the earlier parts of my life didn't come to me during sessions with Doctor A, even when he dimmed the room and put his hands on my head like a charlatan. All I did was sweat until my eyes stung and my skin was clammy.

Tell me about your journey to the city, Doctor A asked me, leafing through his notes. The journey where your life began.

Nice try, it was my turn to say.

I never spoke about that to him. Not even about the swooping of bats, their fingernail-scrape sound still just audible to me back then. Not about watching a group of tiny frogs running across the road one early morning for a full ten minutes, my own survival suddenly thrown into perspective. I had to hold on to some things. They weren't important to anyone but me. They contained no mystery to unlock, they were not clinically significant. They were just there.

Do you ever think you might be too manipulative to treat? Doctor A asked, pleasantly, like I had a choice about seeing him. He met my eyes.

I mean, who isn't, I replied, equally pleasantly. This was the sort of rapport we had established. He took his glasses off.

You seem unstable, he said. You are drinking too much because you are very unhappy. You know that the body possesses its own feedback loops. And you know that you're driving them through your own negative actions. You make things worse and worse. And then what happens?

You tell me, I said.

Doctor A was in one of his stern moods. I wished he would be smiling and indulgent instead. I wished he would offer me one of the red-striped peppermints in the glass dish on the coffee table between us. The window was open a crack and I could hear traffic outside in the distance, a humming beyond preternatural stillness. He wrote down something on his pad. I watched the dictaphone as it spun, taking down every word I said, every word I had ever said to him in this light green room, and felt faint, suspended.

My unhappiness is a long time behind me, I said. My unhappiness is a skin that I have shucked off.

Unhappiness is cyclical, he said. Do not let your heart grow complacent. You won't ever be immune to it. Nobody is.

Sometimes our practice was like a sport. I enjoyed trying to beat him, though I knew I never could. And sometimes I sagged in the middle like an old mattress, and just could not take any more.

He looked up at me. You're very pale, he said. I can read your mood in your skin. Think about what your body is telling you.

He passed me a tissue and I held it in my fist, let my eyes water a little.

That's good, he said. Get it out of you. He handed me the piece of paper. See you on Thursday, he said, and then the session was over and I almost ran out to the car, pressed my head against the steering wheel once I was safely inside.

5

The first time I brought R back to the low white house in the suburbs, I knew that all my neighbours would be at their windows, watching, ready to nudge me in the side when they saw me outside the house or on the green in the coming days.

Nice tall man, they were going to say. What happened to the last one?

In the kitchen I poured equal parts vodka and juice, to accelerate things. Umbrellas on the side of the highball glasses for romance. I put the small bunch of freesias that he brought me in the now-empty vodka bottle, rinsed. In the living room he had taken off his tie and his jacket and laid them neatly over the back of a wooden chair. I liked his manners, the nice swell of his arms, and when he took the drink I liked his smile too. I hoped he would pass them all on to our child. The thought made my heart freeze with alarm.

We talked for a while about work. He asked about the experiments I was working on and I said that they were confidential, which was basically a lie, but I didn't feel like talking about myself. He worked in one of the high glass buildings on the other side of the city and lived near his office in another, similar building. While he explained what he did he was animated and beautiful, but I couldn't listen properly, I couldn't let another second pass. I went over to him and sat on his lap and kissed him. Oh, he said, putting his arms around me.

We took our second drinks to the bedroom. He became simultaneously businesslike and seductive as he unbuttoned then scooped the dress from my body, cursory admiration, pulling out a prophylactic in its little foil wrapper from his wallet before things went too far. He put it on the table next to the bed.

You don't have to, I said.

I will, I will, he said, magnanimously, taking off his shirt.

Part of me was afraid he would somehow sense the dark feeling where it moved under my skin. Sometimes before I slept I put my hands on my stomach and felt a deep pulse that I was sure must be its visible manifestation, but when I read up on this, surreptitiously, it turned out it was just an artery that kept me alive.

I tried to be demure but it wasn't really possible. I couldn't help that I was a person with an appetite. Once or twice there was the threat of warmth, of connection, when he kissed the side of my head, and I didn't want to like it, I knew liking it would bring its own problems. He stayed the night and didn't bother with a prophylactic the second time, or the third time when we woke up. The act itself was vigorous, like doing aerobics. Afterwards I felt healthy as opposed to abject, my body humming softly. In the morning he left early and I didn't mind at all, I preferred it that way.

But after he'd gone I found myself not getting ready for work, instead filling a sock with flour to approximate the weight and feel of a baby's leg. I had never held a baby's leg in my hand, but my heart knew the sensation it was after. I had seen photographs.

I lay prone on my bathroom floor, thinking the forbidden thought *I want to die*, though I was not sure it was true. True and false were no longer opposing binaries. My body was speaking to me in a language I had not heard before.

I knew objectively that to want the small flame of your life to do anything other than what had been given to you was unthinkable, but here I was anyway, doing it. I did not know what they did to the women who got pregnant illegally, though I assumed there must be others out there, I couldn't be the only one. Was motherhood something that could be halted on command, something they could compel out of you once discovered? Was it something you had to see through regardless? I had not lived a life of complete badness, and I wanted to believe that might make a difference, but I knew it would not. There was no way to change your ticket.

When I tried out the words *I have attempted not to want it but I can't help myself*, they felt so good that I said them again, and then again. Please remember that I was not a survivalist, or someone instinctively good at being alive. Please understand that lots of mistakes were made, and some of them were necessary.

Nice tall man, said my neighbour Iona the minute I went outside. She fell into step with me and sparked up her own cigarette, held out the flame so I could light mine. What happened to the last one?

I killed him, Iona, I said to her. He's buried underneath the apple tree. Dig it up if you don't believe me.

Inhale, exhale. A little break from caring. My want had been cracked open. Now I'd have to look inside and see what it contained. Now I had really gone and done it.

She laughed. Oh, you're awful, aren't you!

I agreed. I blew smoke out into the air.

6

I was early for my water aerobics class, so I bought a plastic cup of weak juice and sat in the café. From my table I could not see the children's swimming session, babies bussed in from elsewhere in the city, the more docile suburbs where white-ticket women and their families flocked, but I could hear their heartbreaking noises. Another woman that I did not know caught my eye and grimaced at the sound.

What a racket, she said.

Yes, I agreed.

Glad I don't have to deal with *that*, the woman said. She returned serenely to her magazine, to her breakfast. She raised a piece of toast neatly spread with peanut butter to her mouth. She seemed truly happy. Her skin was smooth, her clothes seemed expensive. I wondered what she might do afterwards with her day, where she worked, what her house was like, whether she was bound to anyone or anything, whether she was thankful for her freedom.

Maybe her day looked like mine. Before coming to the class I had spent some time on an interesting paper for work, scrubbed the bathroom, floor to ceiling, with diluted bleach, so everything was clean the way I liked it. Later I intended to get down on my knees and crawl around for R in the living room, right there where a baby might, in another world, flail and pick things up to chew. We would drink fancy vermouth and it didn't matter if I drank enough to throw up, if I drank enough to ruin the next day, because there were days and days afterwards, endless days marked only by my choices. I had walked to the train station with a spring in my step. My time belonged to me, my life was only mine.

Now, hearing the noises of the children, that all evaporated. A trigger, a reflex. I dug my fingernails into my palms and drank the juice down. But I avoided tears – by now I was used to this intrusion before our sessions in the pool. It was a matter of desensitization. The dark feeling swelled in my chest like a balloon.

Nearer the water, when I had changed into my black lycra costume, I saw some of the children lagging in the pool. They were very small. They laughed and laughed. The chlorine got me right at the back of the throat. I forgot something, I said to the others in my class, and went back into the changing rooms, into the communal showers, crouching down and hitting the water button with my hand as I did so to disguise the sound of my weeping. By the time I recovered my composure, all of the other women were in the pool.

The lifeguard on his red chair waited for me to get in, too, before pressing the button on the tape player. Music rang out. I moved my arms up, and around, lowered myself under. The women pirouetted next to me, splashing in smooth controlled arcs. When I was under the surface I could see their limbs all around me. It was like being inside a strange animal. When we stood up at the end to be congratulated by the lifeguard, the water streamed from our bodies and we felt cold, under the high and vaulted ceiling; we did not feel alone, we were not alone.

7

Trust is integral to our practice, Doctor A said. Trust that I know you better than you know yourself.

I didn't want to do that necessarily, but there was a certain relief in giving myself over to him. There was a relief in being given permission, the same way there had been relief in knowing that there were some paths my life would not take.

I told him once about how I had thought about becoming a doctor myself, and he had laughed at me. He said that being a doctor required a very specific sort of person, and that, with all due respect, that was not the sort of person I was, but I knew that already, didn't I?

For example, he told me, I was injected with a solution that stopped my heart for ten seconds. As part of my training. So I could technically die and then come back to life.

So you could feel superior to us? I asked.

So I could understand and help you, actually, he replied.

A rare intimacy, among interactions designed to approximate

intimacy. He knew that was my weakness, that I was both repulsed and flattered when he let me in. I couldn't resist.

What did you see? I asked him.

I didn't see anything, he said. It was like being in a room with all the curtains closed. I have never forgotten it. You don't want to be in that room.

But what if I'm already in that room?

I think he smiled at that, but his reddish facial hair was longer than usual, obscuring most of his mouth, so it was hard to tell. I could see that he looked tired. It was difficult to pin an age on Doctor A, but that day I put him at around forty-five. The next time I saw him it would be something different. Sometimes I sat outside in my car waiting for him to emerge from the clinic, but though I saw everybody else leave I never saw him walk out, even when it was dark.

8

R and I settled into a pattern quickly. When I got the train or drove to his part of the city we had sex in his clean, spare apartment and then went down to the cheap restaurant a street away from his building to eat plates of eggs or pasta. In the lift we did not speak but sometimes we looked at each other, maybe even a smile, and sometimes in the lift there was another man who lived in the building and R would say Hello, and I liked to hear his voice when not addressing me. It felt like overhearing a telephone conversation or opening somebody else's mail. I already sensed that I was not going to become a full part of his universe, and had made my peace with it. R cracked his knuckles and adjusted his collar in the mirrored wall of the lift, every time. I thought how these insignificant quirks of physical routine built up eventually into a reluctant intimacy, whether you wanted them to or not. I watched my reflection beside his. We looked very good together. We ate our food like we hadn't eaten in years, our knees occasionally jostling under the precarious wooden table.

He came to act less respectfully with me fairly soon. No more talk of prophylactics, for example. I started to mind a little, even though it was part of my plan. It would have been nice to have some sort of feinting towards love, even when he was telling me in bed, breathlessly, that I was a worthless slut. Instead I just responded, More.

More! The proclamation of my entire life. I could be very agreeable, when I wanted to be.

He came to my house too. In my bed I felt the imprints of other blue-ticket women on his body, as if he had absorbed them; what they liked, how they behaved. I wondered where they were, those women past or present, how they had ended up in his arms. You must pay the bill of grief coming your way, I told myself every time he went home at night. The house empty. The neighbours still asleep in the houses around. Each time, I raised my legs above my head, planted my feet on the wall above the headboard. Gravity could not be altered. Gravity was on my side. Then in the morning there would be dirty footprints above the bed – very faint, but still there – and every time they were heartbreaking to me, as if they belonged to my ghost, as if they belonged to me in a different world.

We went away, as a treat, to one of the love motels that everyone used. It wasn't really a trip, only a little way out of the city. You could still see all the downtown lights from the balcony outside our room, where we chain-smoked in between fucking. The room itself was shabby white, pale pink covers on the bed and a plywood headboard painted with red and blue birds. I counted three cigarette burns on the duvet and lay down on my front, underneath it. He buried his face in my neck. You're lovely, you're beautiful, he said. They were just words. They were just sounds coming from a mouth.

He had brought a plastic bag of beers, clinking gracefully. We filled the bathtub with cold water, the bottles, and ice we ordered from downstairs. When we were drunk I took out one of the bottles and wrapped it in a hand towel as if it were a baby. He did not seem to find it funny, but we still drank the baby-beer, passing it between us until it was gone.

He spoke a little about his journey into the city. It sounded like a camping trip. The boys teamed up. Sometimes groups fought other groups. I was the tallest and the strongest, he explained. I considered myself a man already. There was nothing really in my way.

We didn't have the lottery, but don't think it was easy for us. There was a note of hurt pride in his voice. Perhaps we passed on the same road.

I hope not, I said, and he laughed.

I know what the boys do on that road, I didn't say.

The beer stripped me of any inhibitions. I forgot about everything else except our bodies and knelt down on the floor, stretched my arms out over my head. Felt my hair fall everywhere, pulled from where I had tied it up. Pillow at my face. Hand at my neck, thumb right in its hollow. Physical action followed physical action. He pulled out and finished on my stomach and didn't do anything to clean it up, switched on the television, laughed at an advert. I just lay there until it dried, taking pleasure in being unclean.

But later, I pinned him sweetly to the bed with my hands. My body moved and moved. Stay with me, I told him. Stay right where you are. The fringed light fitting above us rattled. He slapped a satisfied hand on to my thigh. I waited until he was soft before I let myself lie down.

When he was asleep I watched the lights from the cars on the road outside move over the ceiling, over and over and over, stroking the little smooth spot of my clavicle where his hand had pressed too hard. That spot was his favourite part of me and I couldn't see why, what had made him fixate on this unassuming piece of bone among all the things that made me up. I had an idea it might be about fragility, and so I didn't want to ask, I didn't want to be disappointed or to disappoint, for I was not fragile, I was not protectable, I was dark wind and dust blowing across a landscape, and there was nothing anybody could do for me.

I looked inside the cool shell of myself for guilt, and found nothing. Only my heart, tense as a fist. My thighs wet. I might have been pregnant already. There's no way of telling now.

9

I knew that my bleed would stop if I was pregnant. That was the only thing I had been able to pick up across all the years of my adulthood, and even that could have been an urban legend. I bled as usual the first month. But when it was time for the second, there was a missed day. Then two, three, four. A queasy count. Ten. Eleven. Like hide and seek, or staying underwater during my swimming routine. I was hoping and not-hoping. I was indifferent. No; that's a lie. I wasn't indifferent at all. But to admit how much I wanted it was a shame even I couldn't articulate. My mind tuned it out like static when I tried. So I just counted instead. Blameless, abstract numbers.

Fifteen. Sixteen.

My supervisor came to watch me squeezing a pipette of silver nitrate into a beaker of water. It dissolved almost at once. Lunar caustic, she said. That's what they used to call it. Very beautiful.

You're a poet, I said. I pushed my goggles up, careful not to touch my face, my eyes.

I had entered chemistry because of the comfort in it. Because you produced a specific outcome, a result known because the combination of substances had been tested many times before, because other people had carried out exactly the same procedure. Of course, you had to be careful about contamination, about the slight fluctuations that could tip the whole process off balance, into something else entirely. But I loved the repetition, the sense of something elemental at work, and the ability of science to explain itself.

Sometimes my life felt like a faulty experiment. I followed all the instructions and yet I did not turn out to be the person I should have been. That was the problem with biology, I supposed, that it was a more inexact field – *the bad science* I had started to think of it privately, spitefully, but only because it didn't go my way. True, I was not as careful with myself as I was with the materials in the lab. In the lab everything had its place, everything depended on the equilibrium of correct labels, cleanliness. Safe handlings and protocols. Rooms where only those with certain privileges could go.

Not a people person, are you, Doctor A had said once, our first or second session. I had wished to be offended, but could not summon it.

The numbers built up. I repeated them over and over, pumping foamed chemical soap in between experiments and lathering it carefully over my palms.

Twenty. Twenty-one. Twenty-two.

10

You seem different, Doctor A said to me. You're nervous. It's like someone has told you a secret and asked you to keep it from me. What could this be, I wonder.

I'm fine, I said.

He got me to breathe into a spirometer to check the capacity of my lungs. I blew until my face was red and the room spun. He took my temperature with a thermometer that went into my ear and bleeped. I prayed for no blood test, no urine test, no palpation of my stomach, no internal exam.

Everything appears to be in order, he said. We'll just have to wait and see. He leaned forward. How often are you thinking about your family, lately?

Not often at all, I told him. I'm coping fantastically with everything.

Doctor A smiled at me. Good girl, he said. Look at you, doing so well.

I I

In the bars after work, my body felt different. Alcohol tasted metallic, as if somebody had dropped a coin in my drink. It acted on me quicker. I started drinking gin and tonics rather than wine because I thought the quinine might be healthy. Cigarettes started making me feel sick, and I didn't like to think of smoke curling around the organs and veins of my new, strange body. One night, my colleagues spoke about summer holidays, asking me where I was going. I said that I hadn't decided yet. Maybe I'll try for a visa this year, I said, and the second the words were out of my mouth I hated myself for saying them, for wanting to brush up against risk even here, like a cat with a post.

I caught sight of R. He waved, walked over and kissed my cheek. It felt good. We moved on to another place, the bar where we'd met, and we sat at the table we had that first night, but neither of us acknowledged it. Maybe he was too drunk to remember. Maybe I had made it up. I picked a small fight in retaliation, because what was meaningful to me was not necessarily meaningful to him, but mainly because there was a part of him literally inside me, growing, and he didn't know.

Why do you need proof of everything? R asked me at the end of the argument. Why can't you live in the present moment? But even the present moment seemed too slippery to rely on. Suddenly the change in me was unbearable.

What do you want to do with your life? I asked. I was looking at him and he was looking at me, but not really looking, not seeing.

What's there to do? he replied.

I don't know, I said, suddenly overwhelmed – desperately wanting to lay my head down on the table, feel my cheek make contact with a hard surface, puddled beer. I stayed upright.

Cheer up, he said. Everything's fine and we're having fun. A song came on that he liked and he nodded his head hard to the beat. He surveyed the room and I surveyed him: the surprising tenderness I felt at the shape of his ear, the part of his hair that was greying, how decisively he held the glass containing his drink. These were things I might contain now. I'm sorry, I said, but he wasn't listening.

My dreams were as vivid as being hit with water. They were edged with a crystal menace that I thought might itself be a symptom. That it confirmed I had the dreams of two people inside me now, and of course the dreams of a child would be as fresh and as strange as this, wet with colour and hung out to dry like a photograph on a line.

In my dreams sometimes I was the girl walking along the deserted road towards the city, and sometimes the girl in pale blue satin walking into the forest, then in the car, keeping silent as the miles were eaten up. In my dreams sometimes I chased the girl and ripped the locket from her neck. Other times I knelt in the slush of the leaves and held my hands out in supplication. Other times I threw myself out of the car. Please, I begged, every time. Please.

Or I was back alone in the bathroom of my father's house, or in the forest and filling my hands with the pine needles, and my body was not changing, and my future was still in everything – the countryside scent, the other clapboard houses, the rabbits whose bodies beat inside the traps.

The next morning I threw up upon waking, though I hadn't drunk so much, doing it very quietly so that R would not hear. I will bide my time, I told my reflection in the mirror. It was a Saturday and I walked back home through the city, too early. There was a scoured, ascetic purity to the deserted pavements, to the absence of noise. The sky was an ugly pink, and the glass towers reflected it. It looked like the sky was bleeding. The entire world was bleeding, apart from me.

1 2

You have two ways to do this, said Doctor A, the day he found out. He had asked me for the date of my last bleed, and I hesitated. He had me lie down on the white-papered examination table while he felt my abdomen, and then he gave me a paper gown and told me to get undressed. My body slicked up with cold jelly, he scanned me with the small probe, from the heart downwards. Liver, stomach, kidneys. The screen was turned away from me. He frowned, pressed buttons, looked closer at whatever images were being transmitted. It was only a matter of time. I pictured the electricity of my heart jumping, the sea-noises of it steady, rapid. I prayed for the baby to stay still if it knew what was best for it, but it turned out the baby would not, could not.

In the waiting room beforehand I had put my head between my knees momentarily, and then staggered to the bathroom to throw up. It seemed that the baby was making me sick, poisoning me from the inside like a virus. The thought was alarming. I made half-hearted peace with the idea of dying there, in the cubicle, bile burning my throat. The clattering feet of impatient women waiting for me to be done, their eyebrows raised when I got out, wiping my mouth. Women would be the ones who knew. Women were my enemies now. My dress was a billowing cornflower-coloured cotton, a disguise that definitely wasn't necessary yet, but I felt compelled to hide my body. Just in case.

After wiping the sweat and jelly from my body with paper towels, I came out from behind the curtain and sat in my usual place. He took a sip from his herbal tea, and mist fogged his glasses temporarily. My fingers pushed the beads of the painted abacus he kept on the table between us. Green, red, blue, yellow. One two, one two. Brown carpet. The institutional orange plastic of my chair. The dictaphone whirred.

I closed my eyes, waiting for him to do something, for someone to break down the door and arrest me, but nothing happened.

Choose now, he said eventually. Opening my eyes, I could see that he looked solemn, but that part of him was also enjoying feeling so important.

Let me take care of it here, today, and you can walk back into your life like nothing happened. You'll wake up and we'll forget all about it.

What's the other option? I said.

I'm not going to force you to get rid of it, but we can't let you keep it either. You'll have to go. You'll be sent away.

Sent where?

He frowned. I can't tell you that, Calla. But I can tell you that you don't want to be on that journey.

I made no move.

Listen to me, Calla. How many chances do you get to make a fatal mistake and have it reversed – forgiven? They'll come for you. There's no escaping it.

He leaned forward and kept talking but I was distracted by the smell of my own sweat. The choice seemed simple and yet the wrong answer was pulsing in me. The hour was almost over. I made a pact with myself to stay silent until the minute hand crossed the line. Finally, he stopped staring at me.

Very well. You can go home. But you'll be under observation from now on, he said. So don't do anything stupid.

13

Come and get me, I pleaded to R on the telephone, ringing him from the box outside the clinic. I want someone to come and get me.

Really? he said. Didn't you drive yourself there? It's not up to me to make you helpless.

His voice was very pleasant, reasonable.

But I need you, I said. Right now, I need you.

I'm really tied up, he said, and so I drove the car myself to his apartment through the packed-out city traffic. I leaned against the mirrored wall of the lift all the way up, eyes closed. Nobody else got in.

It took a while for him to open the door. He was in a pale linen shirt, no tie, and did not kiss me on the cheek or stroke my forehead or look me in the eye or ask if I felt any better, but he did hand me a glass of water with ice.

Rough session?

I drank the water in one go with my fist curled against my chest.

Do you ever want to be a father? I asked him, which was as close as I could get to broaching the dark feeling, how it pulsed in me, what it had made me do.

He leaned against the counter thoughtfully. Oh, is this what this is about, he said, and I was scared for a second, but then he said, You think I'm going to go after a white-ticket?

Well, maybe, I said. One day.

I don't think we should have that conversation right now, he said. Come on.

He smiled, kissed me on the temple and then led me to his room, where he tucked me up in the grey sheets of his bed. Take a nap, everything feels better after a nap, he said, running his hand chastely over the covered lump of my torso. I fell into a hard, clean sleep, a sleep of emotional nothingness, and when I woke up he was gone. I stared at the ceiling for a while, trying to keep hold of the feeling of being emptied out. Afterwards I checked every room, then I let myself out and drove with the radio playing loudly so I didn't have to be alone.

I parked in the city centre and walked around, hoping to see one of the large prams bearing through the crowd. My legs were staggering beneath me. I wanted to see the face of a child, wrinkled and natural as an apple, and the father nodding at the wave of people stepping aside. I wanted proof that it could be done. But no proof was forthcoming.

We all liked to see a baby sometimes. It was traditional to press small offerings upon the father. Coins, sweets, handkerchiefs. The father put them all into a net bag but we knew that they would be vetted later, weeding out anything that could cause damage to the baby.

There were people who might wish to hurt a baby. We could only indirectly acknowledge this. Some women would stare and stare and try to touch the pram for luck. Others were more ambivalent, and some actively avoided being caught up in the knot of people watching, offering, trailing behind. Some did not want to see it.

The first time I saw a baby in the city it was just a curiosity, like something that had come from outer space. But as I got older, babies seemed to become malevolent with their power. They had the ability to undo me. If I saw a pram and gave whatever silver coin I had in my pocket to the father, and he nodded at me graciously, I would have to retreat to the nearest private space and hold myself until the urge to howl subsided.

I went into a shop full of baby things, empty except for the woman behind the counter, who stared at me but didn't say anything. I ran my hands over absurdly small socks, stuffed toys. I picked up a hat with cat ears attached. The blood was hot and rushing in my head.

Excuse me, the woman said, coming towards me. I think you should leave.

But I'm buying something for a friend! I said to her, outraged. I can look, can't I?

You don't have friends like that, she said, so I threw the hat down and walked out of the shop and back into the crowd of people as fast as I could. Stupid bitch! I shouted behind me and everybody looked at me, then looked away.

You think that you are doing the natural thing, but you are wrong, Doctor A had warned me. You think that it's for you but I promise you, it's not.

The streets were clean and grey as I walked, and it was cold. The blossom was not yet out but I knew it wouldn't be long, that there was clockwork ticking inside the sour green buds, because that was what time did. Meanwhile there were no babies in the city today and every-body was going somewhere, sleek and easy as water. I could picture R pushing one of the prams around my neighbourhood, around the streets of the city, while our neighbours tried to get a proper look at the baby. The thought of it made me sit down on a bench and put my head between my knees.

Are you all right? a voice asked.

I looked up at the man and wondered if he was a father. I couldn't look at any man without wondering it. What made a father? What made a mother? What was the thing I was lacking? R was holding out for somebody who would not crawl around on the floor, for some-one who would not heap dirt upon themselves. I was like a baby myself, all sensation, no discipline. A broken engine thrumming with need. I didn't even love him, I didn't love anything.

But also maybe I did love him and just didn't want to admit it. How could I be a mother when even simple human emotions were beyond me, when they were just waves crashing on the shore of my body – this body which at once felt distant as the moon and uncomfortably close? I had not realized it would be like this. I had been stupid not to realize it.

Are you all right? he asked again.

Yes, I said, but I had forgotten the question. The man moved on without comment. I caught the shine of a wedding ring on his hand. My mouth filled with bile. I got up very carefully and walked to the car.

14

The pack came to my door three days after I had spoken to Doctor A.

An emissary rang my bell very early. I saw him through the window and almost bolted, but when I plucked up the courage to open the door he did not arrest me or say anything at all, just handed over the pack and nodded. In the light, the grass looked flat as paint. The deal had been broken. I understood for perhaps the first time that there was no going back, that there was no halting whatever I had put in motion.

I unpacked everything on the floor of the living room and observed it for a while without moving. One small tent, a magic-trick tent, the type you shake out rather than assemble with ropes and pegs. A rudimentary map, eight packets of noodles and four of dehydrated meat, iodine tablets, a small knife, and a pistol that looked very old, antique even. Implements of basic survival. I repacked it all and placed the rucksack in the spare bedroom, on top of the covers, where it lay bright and wrapped in red nylon. Four times on that first day, I checked on it to make sure it had not been a dream.

At least they gave me a tent this time, even if the other objects seemed mostly tokens.

I am going once more on a journey, I told myself. I am going on a great adventure.

15

Nobody has ever done this to me before! R exclaimed in the restaurant where I broke the news to him. It had been over a fortnight since we had seen each other. I chewed my steak neatly and didn't respond right away. I was craving heavy foods, iron-rich, things that bled.

You always wanted to do it, didn't you, he accused me. You wanted to see what it felt like.

What it felt like: cold electricity. A dragging in my body. I felt like a bird that had been pulled, inexplicably, to the ground. A white one with soft plumage, something more beautiful than I can give myself credit for.

Don't make a scene, I said. That's why I brought you here.

Why had I even told him? I could not remember my reasoning. Things kept getting away from me. A golden parrot in a cage shrieked from the corner. A black piano. A waitress in a long navy apron hovered nearby. Everything all right? she asked, and R waved her away with his fork. His face was hard and mean.

Why? he asked. That's all I want to know. Why?

But I could not speak my want aloud – could not send it out into the world and see it bruised, shot down, like it was a debate topic. It wasn't something theoretical, it was a tender wordless part of me, and I had no language for it.

So you're just going to sit there, he said. You're not even going to try to explain yourself.

You wouldn't understand, I said.

You have an emotional disease, he said.

If you like, I said. I could see by the way he was looking at me that any reason would sound wrong coming from my blue-ticket mouth anyway.

I don't know why anyone has a child at all, blue or white ticket, he said, lowering his voice so nobody would hear what we were talking about.

Perhaps nobody really knows, I said. It's a thing you have to feel.

But how do you know that's what you're feeling? Try out some other feelings. Something that you can come back from. He tried to pour me more wine but I'd had too much anyway, I put my hand over the glass. Too late. The wine went everywhere.

I just know, I said. How to explain the dark feeling without opening my whole self up? How to ask whether he had ever felt it too? He was staring at me. I felt pathetic. I licked the wine from the back of my hand.

You know you'll either have to have it sorted out, or you'll be sent away, he said, turning his attention back to his food.

It's too late for that, I said, mopping at the wine with my napkin. I told him about the pack. It's at my house right now. You can come and see it for yourself.

Two pistachio custards were placed before us. I ate them both as R watched. My appetite was enormous. I felt no shame about it, for once.

At my house we laid out everything the pack contained. He lifted the gun in his hand. He pointed it at me. I put my hand to the barrel and moved it away. No, I said, like you would to a misbehaving dog, though I knew it was not loaded. I lifted up my arms to take off my top, but he turned away from me.

I can't even look at you, he said.

I'm starting to show. You can see it now, I said. If you want to.

I was hardly showing at all, really, but I breathed out to exaggerate any bump that was there. I wanted to make it real to him. Something he could see and touch.

I don't want to, he said, still facing away. That's the last thing I want.

He didn't turn around when I slipped off my skirt and then unhooked my bra and rolled my stockings down, slowly, though he could hear me doing it. I said nothing to him, just folded the clothes up neatly and put them on the bed, cupped the very slight curve of my stomach, nothing noticeable, nothing you would see if you weren't looking for it. He kept his arms crossed and his body angled away from me.

Then he left the house. I heard him walk down the stairs one by one, and I did not run after him or make any move at all. I just waited, naked, as the darkness fell and my neighbours returned to their homes. The sounds of their televisions and cooking and doors opening as they went out into their gardens to look at the sky or take the washing in, the small and rhythmic elements of life happening all around me, not-inconsequential life, all of it going on and on.

16

In my next session with Doctor A, I was silent. This time he sat on the brown velour sofa, reclining slightly. It was supposed to put me at ease but I was rarely at ease in his presence, even after so much time, so many years of my life poured out to him. My fingers curled around the edge of the plastic chair's seat, white-knuckling.

If I could fill up the space intended for confessions with inconsequential statements then maybe something could be delayed. I believed that, even though it was stupid, because of course Doctor A knew about the pack, he had ordered it himself.

He smiled and leaned forward as if he had trapped me, though I had not said anything. What's your mind doing lately? he asked me. The usual question.

The light was thin and skittish. Whenever I lied to him I fixed my gaze on the constellation of small freckles below his left eye, or on his nose, which I knew looked like making eye contact. But this time the lie would not come. My stomach growled and broke the tension. Doctor A laughed. Hungry? He offered me a peppermint. My teeth broke the sugar disc at once and my mouth flooded with saliva, so much it felt like it would run out.

Did you receive something, Calla? he said. Has something come to your door?

I didn't speak, switching my eyes to the window instead, the blinds pulled half down, so that the sun came through in slices.

Fear of being banished is an intrinsic human fear, he said. It confirms our status as something other, something unredeemable, which is a suspicion we always have about ourselves. To be banished is to see the abjection latent in you recognized.

He paused. Maybe you want to see it recognized.

Maybe I want to see it recognized, I agreed silently.

Be ready to go at any minute. Keep the pack in your car. The summons will come and it will come at any time, and then you must go. If they catch you, I can't help you. He paused. In recognition of your good service, they will give you a chance. I'm sorry that it has to be this way, he said, and he really did seem to mean it, for a minute.

My breath caught. Another chance at the lottery?

No. You know better than that, he said, shaking his head. What would be the point? It would come out the same. You can't change your ticket.

I imagined myself grown but back there in the lottery station with the gown-clad girls, standing in the line as if I deserved it. I remembered the recurring dream I'd had since adolescence, where I cut my palm open on a sheet of metal and out of my wounds oozed not blood, but an ink-like substance the colour of deep indigo.

A chance to escape, he continued. A journey, I suppose, like your last one. But running away, instead of towards. Some people think of it like a test.

Tell me what to do and I'll do it, I said.

It's a little too late for that, he said. You can only do your best.

I wept to hear his answer, kind as it was, because he sounded so truly disappointed in me for the first time ever.

Do you have a family? I asked when I stopped crying.

I can't talk about that with you, he said. Sorry.

Later R came over when I called. It was unexpected, the acquiescence, but I was grateful for it. He came with a bag of food – shining vegetables, good cheeses, a loaf of the bread I liked.

What are you doing? I asked as he set everything on the table – plates and cutlery and a jug of water with ice and lemon.

I'm trying something out, he said, positioning a knife next to the plated bread. Nasturtiums from the garden in a jar. He checked the label on the cheeses and pointed out the ones I was allowed to eat.

How do you know? I asked.

I managed to find out some things, he said. One of my colleagues gave me this.

He handed me a photocopied leaflet listing foods I should not eat and behaviours I should not engage in. They were all my favourite

64

foods and some of my favourite behaviours. No matter. I would renounce anything. R watched me reading it.

I'll need that back, later, he said.

Could you get into trouble? I asked. I was touched.

Maybe, he said.

You don't need to do anything, I said. I'm a blue-ticket, remember?

I know I don't, he said.

In bed he put both his hands on my face. We looked into each other's eyes properly, holding the gaze. His were so dark they were almost black. I put my hands on his face too. He stroked my cheek, let his thumbs come to rest on my temples.

You're trying something out again, I said, and he nodded.

Looking at him like that provoked a rush of feeling that I resented and embraced simultaneously. It was hard to know if it was real, or just another thing that my body was tricking me into. I realized he was, fundamentally, a good person. This made me feel so sad that I had to look away.

When he was asleep I wrote down *Biochemical reaction!* and *All intimacy is manufactured* in the notebook where I was counting the bloodless days.

Then I wrote *Guard yourself better.* I wrote *Be bold, and be ready.*

17

The supermarket made me feel safe. Even in childhood I had believed that nothing bad could happen in a place of plenty. I loved the relief of the air conditioning, the hyperreal colours under the lights. The supermarket reminded me that my heart was not shrunken and dry yet. The bananas, apples and peaches were arranged in troughs, and a summer smell rose off them. I loved walking around the aisles with my wire basket held loosely in my hand, considering the options, the simplicity of articulating a need and satisfying that need. Salt. Oranges. Strong cheddar. There was a cash machine in the foyer. Every time I visited the supermarket I withdrew money, not too large a sum, nothing to raise suspicion. I kept my body very still as I waited for the crisp notes to come out, inspected my nails as if bored, as if not thinking about a single thing, then when I got home I folded them into the secret places of my rucksack, my jacket.

I stopped by the liquor shop out of habit, remembering too late that I was no longer allowed to indulge this impulse. The owner waved me over with one damp-looking hand. I was a highly valued customer.

Calla, my love. I have a terrific new Beaujolais just in, he said, pouring me some into a paper espresso cup. Try it, you really must.

I tipped it to my mouth after only a brief hesitation, and he refilled it. Beautiful, isn't it?

It tasted like dirt. Lovely, I said, and bought a bottle to pour down the sink later on.

Hide in plain sight, I thought to myself. *This is your fucking life.*

In the pharmacy I collected everything I needed for the month, referring to Doctor A's prescriptions: tinctures, vitamins, dark brown bottles with labels written in barely legible handwriting. The cool and air-conditioned air, my hand on the shelf for balance as I leaned down to take something from near the floor. I felt swollen with my own blood, and everything hurt.

18

One morning, a darker pink smear against pink cotton. Pink on the toilet paper. I sat on the floor of my bathroom and held my hands in fists, very quietly. I counted to a thousand and then counted to a thousand again, told myself, Do not run into the street and howl. Grief overcame me temporarily before I pulled myself back and placed more tissue paper inside my underwear. The day continued. I blamed lack of faith, cosmic instability, the lability of my own fears and thoughts. I checked once an hour. No more pink.

So it could end at any moment, I said to Doctor A. How am I supposed to cope with that?

Yet lots of white-ticket women manage all the time, he said. Interesting.

What if I deserve it? I said to him, like I knew he wanted. What if it's because I'm not suitable?

He stretched out his arms. Time's up, he said. Next patient.

In private moments at home, with the door locked, I rested my clasped hands on my stomach and pushed out. Just to see, I told myself. Three bloodless months gone by. Not so long, really. My lungs, my diaphragm, burned with the strain. I held a pillow under my T-shirt. Just to see. In the mirror in the bathroom I stood on a chair so that I could look at my whole body, headless. I was frightened at the irresponsibility of the act, standing up there on the chair, of how one fall could undo everything.

Part of me considered falling. I am just being truthful. I would fall back into my own life, I thought, just like falling out of my bed after a bad dream. Then I got down very carefully from the chair.

The neighbourhood arts centre was showing a documentary, which I went to see one night with Iona. I had not realized that the documentary was about childbirth. A little reminder of how lucky we were, should we risk forgetting. We watched the hands of the doctors inside a woman's body. Instead of the human sounds they had dubbed classical music over the top. Disgusting, muttered someone on my other side, but I could not see who they were in the dark. Iona passed me a bag of wrapped chocolates, which I waved away. My eyes stayed trained straight ahead.

An emissary on a chair by the door stretched out his legs and yawned, just visible behind the screen. White shirt, navy trousers and jacket, just like anyone else really. I had only once seen an emissary drag a person to the ground, pull them out of view, so quickly that it might not have happened at all, so quickly that nobody could react. Still, I was glad to be wearing a baggy shirt. And I made myself drink from the plastic cup of wine that somebody gave me, despite what I now knew. I wet my lips just barely, smacked them together so they would be darkly stained. During the documentary I hit upon the idea of spilling it down myself. On the screen the woman's mouth was open in a scream of pain that had seemed to last for years, and not hearing it was almost worse, the ridged wetness of her throat visible, and something emerging where the gloved hands of the doctors were dredging. I realized with mounting horror that the same pain lived inside of me, just waiting for a chance to get out.

When the lights came up, people looked at me and the wine all down the front of my clothes. Oh, you've had an accident, Iona said.

She produced tissues from her bag and dabbed at my shirt, my jeans.

I'm so clumsy, I offered up as an apology. I'm so sorry.

Nobody else helped me as I scuffed at the wine mark on the concrete floor with a handful of paper towels. In the air outside, the wet cloth was cold against my skin, clinging to me, as Iona and I walked home in silence.

19

I assumed it was over with R, having not seen or heard from him since the night he made me dinner, but I didn't know for sure until I saw him at the bar one evening after work. He came over to me. I was still attracted to him in a furious way, maybe even more so than before. My hormones were lighting up my blood. Everyone said I looked beautiful.

Before he arrived I had been flirting with a red-haired woman. My hand was on the smooth skin of her bare shoulder and I was laughing. The three of us made stilted conversation for a few minutes before he picked up my coat. Let's go, he said to me. I was thrilled at the presumptuousness of it. The red-haired woman turned away to find a new target.

In my house he heated milk in a small pan, unsmiling. I pawed at him and took off his jacket. I pulled at his belt. Wait, he said, pouring the milk into a cup for me. I drank it obediently and then undid his trousers. I kissed him with my sticky pale mouth. He lay there on the sofa as if he had a headache, staying completely soft even when I stepped out of my dress and got on my knees, even when I draped myself, naked, over a chair.

I can't see you in that way, now, he said, pushing me away. It's just no good. You've ruined it all. He was angry at himself and at me.

I wanted to force tenderness out of him. I wanted to put my arms around him and apologize for what I had done and put my dignity to one side and beg him Please, please, let's work this out together, it's very frightening to be doing this, I don't know what's going to happen to me.

But I didn't – I wasn't capable of being vulnerable for him. Hysteria bubbled up inside me. Instead, I put my white lab coat on over my nakedness. I'm your doctor, I said, giddy. Tell me how you feel, and I'll cure you!

He looked at me. You know, there was a time when I thought I could feel something for you. But not now. Now you disgust me, he said, and then he left. I hammered my fists against the carpet, making no noise at all.

Afterwards I took a long bath and heaped bubbles on top of my stomach. I waited for terror, but none came that night. I dressed in a long soft nightgown and fell asleep peacefully, knowing, finally, that I was alone.

2 0

My neighbours went to Doctor A as well. It wasn't out of choice; he was assigned to us. Our fears and secrets had a geographical trace. You could have pinned them on a map. It was astonishing how he kept it all straight. It was astonishing, too, the idea of him looking into other people's brains. Glowing well-tuned things, so unlike mine, sludgy and stopped-up.

How are you doing? Doctor A asked.

Really well, I lied.

You're lying, he said jovially. There are behaviours that give you away. I won't tell you what they are or you'll stop doing them. Dress off, please.

I slipped my yellow sundress over my head and stood there in my underwear as he measured my stomach with a tape measure. There seemed barely any difference, but it was enough to be quantifiable now. Three inches, he said out loud.

Tell me about your cravings, he said, snapping the measuring tape back into his hand. Tell me about your dreams. His breath was pond-like, yet not unpleasant. I closed my eyes for a second, concentrated on the needling whine of the air conditioning.

Apples, I said. Meat. Dirt.

Dreams or cravings? he asked, and I said Both, and he wrote something down in a notebook. With my back turned to him I put the dress back on, arms catching in the fabric. All along my skin, a thin film of sweat. I thought about killing him, about edging towards his desk and taking up the ornamental letter-opener he kept next to his pens, how easy it would be to do it, but when I turned back around he was looking at me already, and I flushed with guilt.

Keep a dream diary, he said. Write them down. Every single one. Blood pressure time.

He inflated the orange ring around my arm with a rare tenderness, as if fitting an animal for a collar. My arm felt dead, unattached to me, as if it could float away. The air drained from the plastic. The feeling came back.

When do I go? I asked Doctor A again. The waiting is killing me.

He just shook his head. I can't say, he said. It's different for every woman. It's out of my hands now.

This time he had shaved his beard completely off. It was hard to get a handle on his ever-shifting face. Sometimes I wondered if Doctor A was nothing more than a figment of my imagination, a hallucination called up by the smell of new paint and antiseptic.

Do you think I'd make a good wife and mother? I asked Doctor A. Forget about the journey for a second. Forget that I'm a blue-ticket.

No, he said smoothly, with no hesitation, and I was furious. I stood up and knocked the chair over.

You're just proving me even more right, Doctor A said.

Why can't you be kind to me? I said.

That's not my job, he said. What good would I be doing if I just told you what you want to hear?

He righted the chair and indicated that I should sit down, and I wanted to walk out but I sat and buried my face in my palms and let him continue.

That night I dreamed that I gave birth to a stone, and that I put the stone in my mouth and swallowed it, and I woke up ragged with grief. I couldn't write it down.

When Doctor A's receptionist rang me in the week I lied and told her that I had stopped dreaming altogether, that sleep was just a weighted blanket now, and though she made a sceptical noise I stuck to my story. My dreams were between me and me alone. Their shame and strangeness. I have to have something, don't I? I asked my reflection, and she backed me up in silent affirmation.

In the clean spring evenings I spent some time hoarding names. I wrote down words that chimed with something inside me: *Supernova, Mercedes, Desert*. I ran my hands gingerly over produce in the supermarket and turned the names over in my head. *Cherry. Clementine.* Names came back to me in early-morning waking, from everything I had seen in my life, everything drunk up and absorbed. *Lux. Finn. Riley. Dylan.*

I wrote down the names on pieces of paper, chewed the paper and spat it out in the toilet bowl so nobody would see these lists. But that wasn't enough somehow, still tempting fate, so I started interspersing the names with innocent words. *Milk*, I wrote. *Yarn. Chicken.* And even these flat words were named and so had a new worth to them, a new gravity, for it was when considering names that I realized the responsibility, the reality of the act. You could name a child anything.

Pickle, I thought when I looked in the fridge at the jars stacked there, misted with cold. *Rosemary.*

I considered inventing a name, something that had never been heard before. But the world was full of named and catalogued things, and at least by naming the baby after something real I would be tethering them to the world. It was the only normality I could think to gift, apart from love itself.

2 2

Iona fell into step with me as I left the house for work one morning. Her eyes were red and body slack, as if the air were being let out of her. Everything okay? I asked automatically.

She lit up her cigarette. Not at all! she said, blowing out smoke. Romantic trouble. You know how it is. Though perhaps you don't, with that lovely man of yours.

Oh, that's over, I said. She visibly brightened.

Let's get a real coffee, she said, and I hadn't the heart to say no.

In the coffee shop, taking a detour on our way to work, I observed Iona across the white laminated table. My only other friends were the women from the lab, and our friendships were strangely wipe-clean, as if confessions and intimacies under alcohol had no weight the next day. Iona was messy, blotchy with emotion. Her hair fell out of its pins. She was telling me about her latest misadventure, catching a man in bed with someone else, and how could she compete when all the blue-ticket women were just hard-nosed sluts who thought only of fucking. Not you and me, she clarified, we're different, and it's just worse for us because we have standards.

I didn't point out that I had no standards and that in the past I had felt no compunction about borrowing other people. I just drank my coffee.

She stubbed her cigarette out in the crenellated amber ashtray, viciously. He never even took me away for the weekend, she cried. I bet your man did that.

Yes, once, I said. We went to a motel.

Once is enough. I just want to go on a trip! I don't care who takes me, she said. To be taken is the thing.

The more she spoke the more disconnected I felt from everything. The drone of the coffee machine, the silvery sound as I ripped open a sugar packet and poured it into my cup. I wanted to shrink inside my stomach and hide in there with the baby.

It's not so good, I said. It's just another place.

In return I told her that R had left me so that he could pick a woman with a white ticket, and he was going to have a baby that was beautiful and push it around in a big pram. Even though it was a lie I grew weepy and Iona got out of her seat to stroke my back. How dare that imaginary woman have something I could not – how dare she do this to me! The circuits of my rationality were blown. Tears fell into my coffee. Iona lit me a cigarette and I knew I was not supposed to smoke, but I wanted it so badly, so I just tried not to breathe in and stubbed it out when it was two-thirds done. Iona fished it out of the ashtray and finished it off with no shame. I felt sorry for her, and for myself. I was no longer going to be like that – jumping for scraps, scrabbling for them.

I'm just tired of how hard it can be, she said. Her hand went to her locket, a movement reflexive and unconscious. I made the same gesture myself several times a day.

In that same café, another day, I sat alone by the window and drank a cup of hot milk with cinnamon, watching the women and the men go by. White paper bags, spring fashions, hair tied back. I scooped a spoonful of foam from the milk and let it fall to the red table. There was a burn like a wound where the plastic had melted. An emissary was buying a coffee at the counter, but he wasn't watching me. He was tapping his fingers against his navy-clad thigh as if inventing a tune. Even though I had thought often about becoming a doctor, becoming an emissary had never crossed my mind. There were some futures I had never imagined for myself. But then not so long ago this would have been one of them, too.

23

Before I slept, I counted the days. I ticked off another one passed and survived, a tally in the notebook that I hid inside my pillowcase.

One hundred and ten. One hundred and twelve.

The nausea had stopped and I ate tomatoes on buttered bread, jewelled with salt; I ate sliced beef and chicken and tins of sardines too, ravenously. I drank milk by the pint, letting it drip down my front.

When an emissary came into the lab for any reason I awaited the tap on the shoulder, being led out to my car, the horrified faces of the women around me. They were never there for me, always for a meeting with somebody's supervisor or something to do with security, though sometimes I fancied I could see their eyes flicking towards me, as if they already knew.

You look beautiful, the women in the laboratory told me at lunchtime. A group of them came to where I was sitting on a bench outside the building, eating a ham sandwich by myself. They exclaimed over my hair, my skin. They put their clean, dry hands all over me. You're looking so well, they said. We've never seen you looking better. Come out with us tonight, you never come out any more.

I had one drink and poured the rest down the toilet, into plant pots, when I was getting ready. The poor sad fern on the edge of the sink in its green plastic pot. I had murdered it. I was murdering my life. I was creating something new, something bigger than me. It all felt very clear, though I'd only had the one glass to drink. I felt so insignificant, and yet still, there was a universe inside me that nobody knew about. Someone lined my eyes. Someone else stuck a cigarette into my mouth. I coughed and it fell into the wet sink. Let me curl your hair at the front, someone said. I gave my body over to them gladly.

I thought I saw R in the bar, went after him only to find it was someone else with broad shoulders and cropped hair. A city full of men like him, a country full. I would see him at every intersection, every supermarket, for the rest of my life. That was the price I had to pay. Apart from the obvious. In the mirror of the bathroom I barely recognized how good I looked. There was so much smoke everywhere, it was hard to breathe, and I drank my fizzy water and pushed through crowds to where the women were sitting draped around a table, a velvet couch, a blue glass bottle with one single sunflower in it in the centre. They all stared at me but maybe I was imagining it, there were two or more ways to interpret everything, of course I would choose the worst. I sat and did my best to touch their arms and laugh robustly at their jokes. I wanted to be remembered well. I wanted to be remembered at my best.

But increasingly on subsequent days, when I walked about the town, I could sense women gathering at the edge of my vision. Women looking at my body and wondering. They walked a few paces behind me and swapped looks with each other and whispered at the supermarket as I walked past, holding my head high, basket protective in front of my stomach.

In the pool changing rooms, the women watched me too. Iona joined me for water aerobics and she pinched the skin of my waist. The shock of it made me jump away from her.

Surprise! she said.

That hurt, I said.

No it didn't, she said. It couldn't have.

Her eyes were bright. They roamed over my stomach. I took up my towel. I had a vision of them surrounding me in the showers while I sat on the floor with my knees up to my chest, the water coming down.

Afterwards, hair wet in the evening air, I went to my car and saw that one of the wing mirrors had been smashed. Seeing my own face broken that way gave me a falling-away feeling. I drove off as quickly as I could, and when I got home I closed the door behind me and locked it and sank to the floor.

I was leaving them behind – I was saying their lives were not good enough for me. They were right to feel betrayed. I could understand it. And yet at the same time I felt abandoned. The white-ticket women would never accept me. It was lonely to feel like that, a true loneliness. I wanted someone to be happy for me. There was not one person who would be.

24

The summons came before work one morning. While the emissary dropping off the pack had been discreet, there was no need for discretion now. In fact it was better that everybody knew, so that there was no way back. If I tried to return, my law-abiding neighbours would pelt me with vegetables, or worse. I would return to find the windows of my home smashed and my objects ransacked, and if I dared show my face they would drive me away again, or kill me with their bare hands.

A knock at the door came when I was washing up. Then another.

One hundred and twenty-five, I repeated to myself. I leaned over the sink and rinsed my hands. I was already dressed, my hair pulled back tightly. A week ago I had put the pack in the boot of the car, along with my old sleeping bag and a handful of clothes.

I went outside to meet the emissary. He was holding a yellow envelope, sealed. He looked like someone's father, an old and cheerful man who couldn't do anyone any harm. Good morning! he greeted me, handing it over. He took out his cigarettes and lit up with a long wheeze.

The knocking had drawn the interest of my neighbours. They came to their doors in their nightclothes and work clothes, taking in the sleek black car of the emissary, his fresh navy uniform indicating the importance of his visit, and the envelope in my hands. I didn't dare to meet anybody's eyes, not even Iona's, but I heard her exclaim, Calla! What have you gone and done now?

You've got to go at once, the emissary said to me. You get half a day's head start, as an acknowledgement of your good service. He stretched out his arms. Everything about him seemed relaxed. It seemed possible that things weren't as bad as I thought.

There was whispering. I could feel their eyes on my stomach. Someone started to hiss.

Five minutes, he said to me. Don't just stand there.

In the house I opened the envelope, but it was empty. I checked the stove was off and took my car keys from the drawer, picked up the kitchen scissors and my toothbrush and my notebook, slipped my denim jacket on to my shoulders. Congealed yolk on the plate in the sink, a bright smear. I ran back outside to where the emissary was waiting.

Ready? he said, throwing his cigarette to the ground but not stepping on it. That's the spirit. Thanks for making this easy.

The hissing grew as I checked the boot. I couldn't help myself and looked back to find a wall of women, hard-faced, inching past the territory of their front doors. Their feet crossed their thresholds. Some did not have shoes on. The emissary raised his hand as if conducting an orchestra, and they paused, but when I opened the door to the driver's seat they started to surge forward again.

Order, please, the emissary proclaimed. He blew a red whistle shiny as an apple, long and true. I could hear it even with the doors of the car closed, even as I started up the engine. The leather was hot under my legs already. I sweated through the thin fabric of my trousers.

Half a day. Twelve hours. The roads were long and winding. The country was vast. I did not know where I was going. The map was still in the boot. I had to just press my foot to the pedal and go. Someone slapped the bonnet of the car as I started to move, then others slapped the boot, the back window, but I didn't see who. I accelerated. Somebody threw something soft and it hit the car with a thud.

The early-morning glare was dazzling. In the mirror I could see my house was already being swarmed, the home that was mine and only mine, where I should have lived out my days. Nobody was running after me. I pulled out on to the road and was gone in minutes; it was that easy to be banished, it was that easy to leave and be left behind.

Road

I

I filled the car with petrol the first chance I got. Having a car at all was a problem, I knew. There was no emissary in the garage, though there was a security camera that I tried not to look at. There were women before me who had escaped, there must have been, because it was inconceivable that there could not be, because believing in something is the first law of survival.

I drove for hours, taking main roads for speed, though I had no idea whether the promise of the head start was real. In a lay-by, fronded with red dust, I eventually stopped to rest. I placed vitamins under my tongue and then I pushed the driver's seat back all the way and put my head between my knees as if faint, and I started to cry, cringing my body in on itself.

I was a warm-blooded female animal. I was a doll with another doll inside of me. I was the chicken I opened up one day only to discover that the stomach had been left in by mistake, a pearlescent bag still full of grain from its final meal.

On the car's clock, the display told me that soon the twelve hours would be up. Soon there would be emissaries spreading out from the place where I had made my home, looking for a car like mine, a woman like me.

But I had to take some time to cry about my house, my poor house which had not done anything wrong, which was now full of people who hated me and all my belongings destroyed, and while it seemed trivial to cry about material things under the circumstances, all those things had added up to my life, and it was hard to think about that.

I wanted to talk to Doctor A, was almost frantic with the urge. I wanted to be back in the room of the clinic, the sound of the air conditioning full in my ears, but it was too far away, and I was too far apart from everyone already.

After the crying had passed over me I sat in the car with my arms around my knees and watched the farmers tending to their crops in the fields, on their knees with their palms cupped around budding greenery. Heads swooped by in hoods or gauze, protecting them from the pesticides. How good to be a person who grew things, who delved into the soil and waited. It seemed easy.

2

I stopped in a seasonal town, one that would probably be busy with day-trippers by high summer but now lay empty. Plastic rubbish studded the gutters of the main road. Most things were closed, but there was a public bathroom that was still open. I descended its steps and climbed over the turnstile. The floor was wet, as if recently flooded. Warped voices came from the men's toilet, next door, or maybe just one voice that was refracted. The voice or voices did not come closer and soon stopped, which was worse.

There was a perfectly square mirror on the wall, rust-speckled. An idea came to me. I took the kitchen scissors from my bag, twisted my hair in one handful, sawed through it with the blade. My long hair was beautiful where the rest of me wasn't, but I didn't hesitate. It only took a few seconds and then it hung unevenly around my jaw. My head felt much lighter. I left it on the floor for someone else to find, stepping around the dark pelt of myself with great care.

There was one shop open after all, an all-purpose shop, selling everything from milk to screwdrivers. The fluorescent light stammered. In the back, next to some rolls of wrapping paper, I found a packet of stiff white card. It was glossy – card to paint or draw on.

Back in the car, I jumped every time I saw a man or woman dressed in navy. Dark and terrible things crowded at the corners of my vision, always revealing themselves to be a tree, the corner of a house, a shape cut from the sun.

There was a hotel open beyond the next town, on a small and winding road that led further into the mountains. The town of my childhood was further north too, but I would not go back. There were likely emissaries lying in wait there already. My paranoia was like a physical substance, a watercolour paint that tinted everything. And yet I parked the car like it was a normal thing to do, like everything was fine.

A boy with a bloom of acne across his forehead and a red shirt with no tie wrote down R's surname on the register, gave me a gold key. Small act of rebellion. I had always preferred his name. *Sorry, husband,* I thought with satisfaction. I saw nobody in the lift, watched the numbers move until we got to my floor. A chime as we arrived, swirled paisley carpet giving way to square pale tiles in the corridor itself, and only one light on the ceiling working. I walked past eight blue doors. Mine was the last. Around the lock it was scratched as if people had had difficulty opening that door particularly. It opened with a click, and I locked it behind me.

I found a small kettle on the sideboard, filled it and set it to boil. I turned on the taps overhanging the avocado-coloured bath and held my hand under until the water was too hot. The light in the bathroom was too bright but I left it on so I could take an inventory of my body. The water was mineral-tasting when I dunked my head under the surface. Rust stains around the base of the taps. My stomach bobbed up like it was hollow. My hair stuck to my head and neck. There was a scratch on my ankle that I didn't remember getting, and I thought about my own blood and the blood of the baby inside me mingling, whether there was any separation, whether I counted as one or two.

Poor baby, having to drink my blood. I put myself underwater again. I opened my eyes so I could see the light.

I wondered what R was doing. I could not imagine him naked in a bath, so vulnerable, so prone to drowning. I could only imagine him lying on my sofa, deciding that desire stopped there. I wondered if he was laying the groundwork for a life without me — looking for the new woman, somewhere in the city, with clean hands and cold eyes. Perhaps no white-ticket woman would have him, I thought viciously. But I knew that plenty would.

My father had moved from city to country. Better life, he had said. I thought about him and whether he might still be there in the house I had grown up in, going from room to room, sweeping the floor-boards and having his friends over for beers and cards like the old times. Quiet life. Maybe he was dead. I had phoned him once from the city to tell him I had made it there safe. *Safe* had become a relative term. He had said Good, and Take care, and then somehow we had never spoken again, as if now his duty was done. I didn't know if I missed him. I thought about the clear water of adulthood, the mud you had to swim through to get there. The girl in the other room, the only one granted a white ticket. Driving past me in the car, motion-less, saved.

The peach paint of the walls was in need of touching up. I got out of the bath and drew the net curtains. A wave of nausea; I went back into the bathroom and gripped either side of the sink. My hair needed washing. I was sallow in the light. I was thinking only of goodness, and how far away it felt from me. Goodness was a country I could not get to. Goodness did not live in hotel rooms. Goodness was a state of permanence, not like the varying states of my body as it now existed. All the bodies that had passed through this room had left their dents in the mattress and fingerprints on the cups just like I would, left their sadness to accumulate like the dead skin of their dust. How many had been pregnant? The word still felt awful to say. Pregnant! I whispered. I didn't dare speak it louder.

When I was dry and wrapped in a thin clean towel I took an inventory of my belongings. When I emptied my jacket pockets I found a dark red lipstick, a relic from another time. I wanted to write something on the wall, somewhere secret, but was not brave enough. Instead I put it on and observed my new-old face and kissed the mirror, to say *I am here*, then wiped the imprint away. I used the kitchen scissors to cut out a fake white ticket from the packet of card I had bought, using my own blue ticket as reference. It wasn't really any good. My hands shook. I cut another version, then another, both slightly better. I slipped the blue ticket into my wallet, right at the back. In my locket, the white counterfeit. I turned the lights out in the bedroom and opened the curtains for a second to skim the roadside. I thought I saw a dark figure standing in the car park, but as I stared at the shape it faded away.

3

In the morning I felt the eyes of the boy on reception boring into my back as I left, but when I turned he was just leafing through papers. It was possible I was placing too much importance in my badness because, after all, nobody knew what I was yet. I was somebody else temporarily, and actually that was a kind of gift too, I reasoned, because I had always wanted to try on another life, and now I could. I pretended in the car that I was on my way to pick my child up from school, that there was a husband preparing a healthy lunch for us even as I drove, that soon my child was going to leap into the car and tell me they loved me. This child-image was nebulous – I couldn't picture them as anything beyond a shrunken adult, staring baldly at me from the back seat. When I looked into the rear-view mirror I realized I hadn't even brushed my hair that day, and that my overfamiliar face was creased with worry where I had slept awkwardly on the pillow. And, all things considered, the spell was broken.

Driving was monotonous even with the undercurrent of fear, the instinct to run. I switched the radio on then off. I was not totally sure what was expected of me. Every so often I would veer on to another side road, take a circuitous route to make me harder to track. The lack of visible threat was unnerving, lulling, like I was drugged. I was glad when I had made it through another day and decided upon another hotel, set well back from the road. This one was all greens – sage carpet, apple-white walls, darker trim on the panelling. A woman this time on the reception desk, younger than me and sweet, absent-minded, but I think I trusted more the innate obliviousness of men. Doctor A aside, I felt them less able to see into or through me.

In the room, old restlessness. The desire for forward momentum. I went for a walk down the road from the hotel in the gloaming to shake out some of the energy from my bones. Around me the landscape was flat and peaty, lumpen brown grass and fields stretching out. A sheep in the distance raised its head to look at me and didn't stop watching until I had long passed. I missed the clean roads of the suburbs and the order of my own garden, the grass, the seeds into which I had funnelled any earlier motherly instincts.

There was a small bar perhaps half a mile down the road. Inside, the walls were draped with lights flashing red and green, red and green. A sleek blonde woman poured black liquor into very narrow glasses, pushed them down the length of the bar. There were not many people, but those who were there seemed excitable. I slipped in and everyone turned to me. The woman poured me a glass before I could say no. Celebrate with us, she said to me. I took the glass and put it to my lips. It was hot in my throat, tasted of aniseed.

What are you celebrating? I said, confused. The return of the blue fox, a pink-faced man said to me, two heads taller than I was. He knocked his glass against mine. There is a type of fox that comes back to us when the weather warms. It's so beautiful. It's very rare. Nowhere else in the country has a creature like it.

My black jumper disguised the shape of me. I dissolved into the darkness of the bar. Everybody was talking about this fox. Somebody showed me a photograph of it, a square clammy between their hands.

But it's not blue, I said, and everybody laughed as if I had said something hilarious, some people had tears in their eyes. Blue doesn't always mean blue, someone explained to me. Oh, I said, but this statement worried me more than it should have done. I wanted to hang on to the known things, to the facts and the order that governed them.

What's your name? they asked, and I said, Iris. A beautiful name, the people said, and they toasted me.

And your husband? Where is he? asked the barmaid slyly.

He has a headache, I said. He's back at the hotel. And just like that I was a white-ticket woman with a drink in my hand. Just like that, I belonged somewhere. Another life to try on.

I found myself in a corner with a younger man, a woollen scarf the colour of the sky wrapped three times around his neck. He seemed sweet, like a brother. Blue, I said out loud, touching it. All this fuss, he said very quietly to me. Everyone kept laughing at my requests for water. The man had curly black hair and he put his hand, gently, on my forearm. Then he put his arm around me. I didn't want to say anything in case I offended him, he was so friendly after all. The blonde woman watched from behind the bar, polishing the same glass over and over. I excused myself and went to the bathroom, where I tipped the rest of my drink down the sink, refilling the glass with water from the tap. But it was too late and I was drunk already, my body wasn't used to alcohol any more. Sorry, I said to my stomach again. Sorry, sorry. In the merciful amber light of one dying bulb, I redid my lipstick.

The man with the scarf was waiting for me. Come outside, he said urgently, so I followed him out on to the road. The people-sounds from inside bubbled and seethed.

Are you from the city? the man asked me, lighting a cigarette. I nodded. So you don't celebrate the fox festival, he said with satisfaction, breathing out a plume into the air. You likely have no idea what we're on about. You probably think we're uncultured idiots.

I don't think that, I said.

Do you really have a husband? he asked.

Yes, I said.

What's he like? he asked.

I thought for a second. Tall, and very kind, I said.

Great, he said. Well done you.

He took my hands as I stepped backwards to avoid the smoke. Please, anyway, he said, and I knew what he was asking but I was confused, still, as though the whole evening had slices missing from it, like the blackouts that had peppered my first years in the city, the brain processing what it needed to process, and the strangeness of this, of being recalled to another version of myself, caused me to crouch down for a second.

A crowd of people came out from the pub, carrying bottles. Come on, come on, they said. We're going to the party at T's house.

You've got to come too, said the barmaid to me. Come on, let's just have a little fun.

The man with the blue scarf held on to my arm and then let go. Yes, you must, he said. Come on, I'll lead the way.

I have to go back, I said.

No you don't, he said to me, and his smile was very beautiful.

We all walked across the moorland. The moon was high and everything was cold. My body was loose. The voices of everyone talking
and laughing reflected around us. It felt companionable. I was still
drunk. When a broad man with a beard passed me a bottle I drank
from it anyway, just a little. That's right, he said. See, we treat our
guests well.

I wondered if I was purposely masochistic or just a moth blundering
into a flame. I wondered if motherhood held such appeal for me
because it was a masochism you couldn't ever let go of. I turned my
face up to the night.

The party was in a cottage tucked into the moor, surrounded by rocks.
All the lights were on. A thin man opened the door, dark beard growing up his cheekbones. What took you so long, he said. There was a
broken sofa in the front garden among the flowerbeds, the leather of
it seamed and shucked, but people were sitting on it anyway. The
dark-haired man bowed to us extravagantly. Come in then I suppose,
he said. Everyone slapped him on the shoulder. I was the last to go
in. He took my hand, lightly, then dropped it without saying
anything.

There were people inside already, smoke everywhere. This is Iris,
our friend from the city, the barmaid said. We're showing her our
good country hospitality. Not good enough though, where's her
drink?

Glasses passed around, more dark liquid. Drink, they said. You'll
offend our esteemed host if you don't drink. And the man called T

99

was there closing the door and coming deeper into the room. People would not stop talking to me over the music, which was too loud, strings and guitars wavering on a record player. They all knew each other. I started smoking to give me something to do with my hands, I could sense T's eyes on me from all the way across the room, he was wondering who I was, this person who had just walked into his house and was now holding court, silently, smoke in my mouth. I was a little afraid of him, so I did drink, so that he could see me partaking and to make me brave. I didn't like the closed door. Wooden shutters at the window. There was a little white-painted stool in a corner that I sat down on, but this was a mistake, I hemmed myself in.

He came over and took my hand again. He traced his fingertips over my palm and I shivered involuntarily because it had been a while since I had been touched in a way that portended actual intimacy. He leaned into me, too close.

Tell me about yourself, he said. He was very intense. I normally liked that in a man, but I didn't like it then. I blew smoke into his face instead, and he didn't flinch. I'm nothing, I said. There's nothing to me.

The cigarettes were a mistake, it was all a mistake – time blurred and skipped and I was running to the bathroom, pushing past the line of people waiting, and throwing up strings of yellow bile, dark alcohol, into the stained toilet bowl. There was a window, I noted hazily, out of habit. Frosted glass, the sills rotting.

Unlock the door, said a voice. I'm in here! I shouted. Unlock it anyway, they said. You're not well, we'll look after you. I did as I was told. T came in, and the man with the blue scarf, and the barmaid. Are you all right? they asked one by one. They closed the door. I nodded yes and switched on the tap, cupped greyish mineral-tasting water in my hands and drank. When I splashed it on my face it beaded my eyelashes, and all was light. The men looked at each other. Sit on the floor, T said.

The barmaid sat first. Come on, she said. She took my hand softly. The whorls of her fingertips were dirty. I dropped to my heels and she cupped both hands to my head. Her nails found my scalp. I had forgotten already how to be around people, it was so easy and quick to forget. I wanted the comfort of another body but I was too afraid to show myself. T crouched down beside me too. He put a dry hand on my forehead and then kissed me, hard, on the side of my head. He smelled like smoke and clean paper, and of the beginning of sweat. I tried to move away but he put his arm around my shoulders. Not so fast, he said.

The man with the blue scarf got on to his knees too, pulling up the hem of my dress, plucking at the small holes where my tights were worn, and T copied him. Help! I called out, but at once there was a hand over my mouth. I pulled down the fabric of my jumper where they were trying to ruck it up. The barmaid let go of my mouth. White-ticket, she said, snorting with laughter. Yes, sure. You're as much a white-ticket as I am. Who are you trying to fool? Look at her stomach. Go on, check, I bet I'm right.

You can't, I said, slowly. You have to let me go.

She held a bottle to her own lips and then to mine, but I didn't swallow this time. Sweet wine rivered down my lips, chin, on to my dress. The man with the blue scarf licked it from my face.

Someone banged on the door of the bathroom. The pocked floor scratched against the backs of my thighs where my dress had rucked up. Fuck off! T shouted. We're busy! The man with the blue scarf was red in the face as if embarrassed by what he was doing; I hit my knees together like clappers and felt them make contact with his elegant knucklebones. He swore and pulled his hands away. T was trying to alternately tug and push me flat on to the floor, but there was a hesitation in his movements that confused me. It almost seemed like an absurd, elaborate joke, but at the same time it was hard to breathe. Come on! the person outside said, laughing and banging again, with such force that the hook popped open and they stumbled into the room. It was another man, fair hair down to his shoulders and a beer in his hand. He surveyed the scene. Sorry to interrupt, he said. The others paused and I took the opportunity to push myself to my feet, palms against the floor. Breathe, I told myself, as the room spun.

Oh, just let her go, said the man with the blue scarf. He held out his hands. Look what you did, he said, wounded, but there was nothing to see.

T threw his hands up. The fair-haired man stayed there, watching. Get out then if you're going to get out, T said, glancing towards him. We were just playing. I made to walk out but he grabbed my ankle and pulled me back, almost toppling me over. I kicked and he laughed, then let go properly, and I escaped back into the other room. The smoke was thicker and the voices were louder. I blundered, mouth sour, out into the front garden where three people were still sitting on the rotting sofa, and then on to the moorland road. The threat receded. Soon I couldn't even see the lights of the cottage behind me.

Back in my hotel, I stuck a chair underneath the handle of the locked bedroom door and put the duvet and pillow from the bed into the bathtub of the en-suite, then locked the bathroom too. All through the night I waited there. I held the pistol between my knees, aimed at the door, until it was too heavy for my wrists.

There was grief in the night, even when I clasped my hands over my stomach. What have you done? I asked myself. It wasn't like my life was unbearable before. There were lots of things I had not been grateful enough for, I saw now. There had been no nights in bathtubs waiting to be caught.

Wanting is a powerful magic, Doctor A had said. Try wanting something else and see how quickly your desires recalibrate once you get it.

But this is different, I had told him then.

The dark feeling there, always there, under the skin, a steady current. Sometimes lulled and weaker but always returning, as if it were a tide.

In the morning I was lousy with guilt and exhaustion. I stripped naked and ran the hot water where I had been lying, wiped a patch clear on the fogged mirror to look at myself. The gentle curvature, the stretched skin, the blue veins widening and wrapping. I'm sorry, I said out loud, tapping my stomach with my fingers. Do you hear me in there? I'm sorry.

When I opened the bathroom door everything was as I had left it. Sunlight streamed through the gap in the curtains. The car park was deserted but I drove away at a great speed anyway. A cloud of dust. The white peaks of the mountains closer to me all the time. The promise of safety, the promise of something.

What if I could not do better? What if I was incapable? What if this was the best I could do, had reached the limit of what I was capable of, so soon, with so far to go?

4

I rang Doctor A from a payphone on the road, giving in to an urge I didn't necessarily want to interrogate. When he heard my voice, Doctor A clicked his tongue as if it were a surprise, but I knew it could not be.

Hi, I said breezily.

So they've come for you, he said.

I mean, you sent them, I said.

He ignored that. We can do our appointments over the phone, until you're caught, he said instead.

What makes you so sure I will be? I asked.

Calla, please, he said, very kindly.

I have reserves that you don't know about, I told him.

You forget that I know everything about you, he said. You don't need to be so angry. There's no harm in being predictable. Even the act of calling me today – I was expecting it. Ring me twice every week at the usual time.

I said I would try.

He said I should do more than try. He said the body and the mind were often in opposition and the importance of keeping them well-tuned and functioning in unison was paramount, as much as was possible, given my condition. He clicked his tongue again. He spoke a lot of sense.

I must go, it's time for my next appointment, he said. But remember that it's open season on women like you. You are a criminal now.

I hung up the phone and leaned against the wall, breathing hard.

In the car, driving again, I listened for my name on the radio, moving the dial compulsively. Weaving in and out of high terrain, the signal skipped and thickened. I was going nowhere fast. Sometimes I would pull over to write down the cars I had seen behind me, in case there was a pattern, in case they were following me. A silver one. A red one. A white one, large, more of a van.

Mostly blue cars, dappled with mud. Blue everywhere. In the plastic detritus by the side of the road, in the curtains of houses that I passed. I paused to pick some berries from a dusty bush at the edge of a lay-by, and got blue juice all over my hands for my trouble. I was in so much trouble. I spat the berries out in a sudden fit of fear that they were poisonous after all, but the taste stayed with me, I feared it would never leave.

As a sea of trees rose on the horizon, a sign indicated a car park. I pulled in for a rest. Nobody else was there. I walked into the forest, over knots of tree and dirt. The ground was wet in places from a brief shower. Somewhere in the distance there came the curved yowl of a bird of prey that I couldn't see. I walked onwards, towards the sound.

On the ground was a dead rabbit, disembowelled. Still fresh, the dark loops of its insides glistening like jam. I knelt and hovered my hands above its fur, checked its eyes for pinkness and swelling. The rabbit's stomach seemed swollen. But then that could have been me again, seeing pregnancy in everything. The rabbit's eyes were milked over but still watched me.

With my bare hands and the knife I dug a shallow hole. There was no ceremony except for laying the rabbit in it and then filling the grave up. There were no words to be said. It was stupid to care about anything.

From the boot of the car I pulled a bottle of water to drink from, to wash my hands. I stared at the other things I was carrying there: the tent, the sleeping bag. I rinsed my filthy hands and broken nails, racked with disgust, and drove on.

5

In a quiet diner as night started to fall I sat in an orange leather booth and waited for something, for anything. A sign, I wished silently to the dark feeling, to the baby. Just tell me what to do. The sky outside was deep violet. The walk from the car to the building had smelled powerfully of rain. A small woman brought me a laminated menu. Sandwiches lay behind glass at the counter, illuminated in a sickly way. On the wall were black-and-white photos of famous people who had died.

There were two other women in the room, one with long black hair and the other fair-haired, greying at the temples. They spoke quietly to each other. The dark-haired woman's face was lean, her lips compressed into a tight line. She was beautiful enough for me to feel jealous of the fair woman, even though I didn't know if they were together. The waitress came back, and I ordered a cappuccino, a stale-looking croissant, though when it arrived I could only break off pieces of the pastry and place them very carefully into my mouth, chew for a while, then spit into a napkin. My eyes kept skidding to the faces of the women, over and over. I tried not to show that I was looking. Other women had become objects of anxiety for me, even the waitress, who wasn't paying attention to the shape of my body, swaddled under loose fabric. I knew I should go but I wanted to watch.

In the bathroom I was washing my hands when the dark-haired

woman came in, the doors swinging behind her. I froze; unfroze. We made eye contact in the mirror. The bathroom was painted an ugly brown, one lamp burning in the corner. Pale tiled floors, with dirt accumulated at the edges. I felt faint, put both my hands on the fake marble counter. The woman kept looking at me in the mirror.

There's something wrong with you, she said.

No, I said, though it was pointless to deny it.

Sit down, she said.

Who the fuck are you? I moved to go, then turned back to face her directly.

I saw you looking at me, she said. What were you looking at?

Her hand was in her pocket. A knife, I thought, stepping back.

Nothing, I said. Can't you just leave me alone?

I felt dizzy. I let myself fold, leaned back against the wall and slid down. She put her hands out to my arms. She knelt on the floor so we were eye to eye. The smell of her hair was overwhelming. Something changed in her eyes.

You are, she said. She indicated a bump with her hands.

No, no, I said, pushing her away.

It's all right, she said to me. Look. She grabbed my hand and placed it on her stomach, intimacy that struck me like a bolt of electricity.

Are you? she asked, indicating my locket. I looked away with shame. It seemed obvious that I had a blue ticket, that if I opened my locket she would see through the counterfeit at once. She didn't make to show me hers.

Where are you going? she asked, lowering her voice, putting her mouth to my ear.

I don't know, I admitted, whispering back into hers. I'm just going.

Wait here, she told me. Don't move at all.

She went into a stall. I got up and washed my hands again for something to do. The skin was reddening and drying out. The nail beds were raw from where I was chewing them constantly, as if I were a teenager again.

The toilet flushed and she emerged, washed her hands next to me. I told you not to move, she said, and I thought it was a joke but she wasn't smiling. We looked at each other in the mirror again, side by side. She was a head smaller than me. Eyes huge and black in her skull.

The border, she said.

She took out a map from her back pocket, an A–Z. It was creased and warm from her body. She unfolded it and showed me briefly – an orange line, slightly thicker than the others, near the edge of the paper, indicating change, indicating before and after. Do you have a map? she asked.

Yes, I said. They gave me one. It's in the car.

She raised her eyebrows. Next to her I felt soft and stupid. I felt like someone who should have been killed a long time ago.

It will be out of date, she said. Buy a new one. The most recent edition you can find. Then you just go north.

Wait, I said. I didn't want her to leave, but she was already turning away.

I have to go, she said. Good luck.

What's your name? I asked her. I'm Calla.

She surveyed me. Marisol is what I'm calling myself, she said. I'd pick a fake name, if I were you.

I returned to my seat after her, watched the two of them get up and leave, still talking urgently. The fair-haired woman stared at me as they moved past my table, so she must have noticed me looking too. I kept my eyes on the table so she would know I wasn't a threat. It was almost black outside now, but I didn't have anywhere to go or be. The woman behind the counter turned off the coffee machine, the light of the glass sandwich cabinet, started wiping down the surfaces. She reluctantly showed me to a room upstairs when I asked.

When she had left me alone I listed things that I had done right. I thought about shelters built on my first journey to the city, scraps of tarpaulin. I thought about wire traps for rabbits. I thought about the efficiency with which I had got myself pregnant. I thought about slowing my breath and hiding so well that nobody could see me, so that I was dead but still there. About jumping into bodies of water and staying under the surface until my lungs burned. I am a creature of instinct, I told myself. I am a creature flinging herself forward. Tomorrow I will make a real plan.

In the night I dreamed of being an animal of the dark, and it was a comfort, for it was confirmation that I belonged. Owls swooped around me, and they were my sisters. The light of the moon cooling, like rain. Then I was galloping, not flying. My body came to rest on wet grass. My mouth nipped at dirt and leaves, my skin was alive, and I was a deer, or a badger, or a mole inside the ground, and I could run for miles.

6

I was still driving and the road was changing all the time, the landscape was changing, I could not get a handle on it. The half-remembered roads, the slips of language, the climate which was familiar and yet not. I had two brains inside of me and two hearts, and the baby-brain and baby-heart wanted to take me over. Tendrils through my blood. Everything was made of glass. It had been like this always and now it was just that I was noticing it, the shimmering precariousness of life, and the death-filled underbelly just out of sight.

Border, I thought, when the panic threatened to take me over. Border.

A sign for a bed and breakfast was nailed on to the side of the road, pointing half a mile down a dirt track. I was in the middle of nowhere again, in spare and rocky alpine country. As I drove down the track, birds threaded the sky above the car. I rolled the window down to get some air. Red rabbit. A field of sunflowers.

The bed and breakfast was a tall mushroom-coloured house set into trees, with a wooden porch and pale blinds. It felt like a place I had been to before, an idea of a place. When I knocked on the door, a woman answered. She was old, her hair cropped close to her head. A room? I asked her. Yes, she said, unsmiling, letting me in.

We walked past wallpaper with a muted floral pattern, the baseboard painted dirty white. A staircase reached up through the centre of the house, a small desk next to it where she thumbed through a guestbook.

Are you busy? I asked her, though it was clear the house was empty.

We're never busy at this time of year, she said to me. Too early still. She peered at me. You're not from here, are you?

No, I said. I'm taking a trip. I'm meeting my husband at the end.

I see, she said. Let's go find your room.

As we climbed the stairs, two cats ran across the landing with a shriek. They stopped when they saw me and the hackles rose on the backs of their necks. I knelt down, tried to put out my hand to them, and they hissed.

In the room she turned to me. Why don't you come down for a cup of tea, or a nightcap?

All right, I said, as if hypnotized.

She withdrew and I sat on the edge of the bed. I kicked my backpack underneath it and lay down fully clothed, even wearing my shoes, with my arms folded across my chest.

The living room smelled damp. Forest-green wallpaper peeled at the top of the wall. The woman had laid out a tray of small pale biscuits and a steaming pot of tea, a dark glass bottle and a small glass next to it. She poured me hot tea into a china cup. For herself she poured tea and also a glass of the liquid in the bottle, which looked like water but was not.

You can't have this, she said. Not in your condition. I made to stand up and leave but she took hold of my arm and pulled me back. Next to her chair I saw a carpet bag, the shine of metal implements inside. My teeth knocked against the cup. She was wearing a locket but did not show me what it held. Follow me, she said. She did not let go of my arm.

The dining-room table was dark, polished wood. I lay flat upon it with an embroidered cushion under the small of my back and another under my head. She was setting out the cold tools, one by one, on a small silver tray like the one that had held our biscuits. Things to lever me open, to do other things. I considered running. A grandfather clock marked the seconds. If she could help, I would give my body over to anything. I would do dark bargain over dark bargain. My arms were bare, my T-shirt rolled up. The woman put on disposable medical gloves, the same brand that Doctor A favoured. She put the orange collar of the blood pressure machine around my arm like so many times before. She did not say the numbers out loud but instead wrote them in a small notebook that lay on the table next to me. She listened to my heart, my stomach, with a stethoscope, and then she straightened up.

Why would you want to do this? She sounded disgusted. Oh, I've seen it all, and yet I still cannot believe it.

The blood rushing to my skull gave me an underwater feeling. I wriggled my toes. You girls, she said. You could have done yourself real damage just taking out the device. Blood poisoning. Your whole body all septic and green. Stupid!

I stared at the ceiling. I agreed with her, privately.

Have you noticed any symptoms? she asked. Are you sick? How about bleeding?

I really do feel fine, I said to her.

I could do the procedure here, she said, looking at me. I can do it right now and you won't feel a thing. It's not too late.

My heart was pounding very fast. My heart moved up, into my mouth. No, I told her.

Fine, she said. I won't push it. It's your body.

Is the baby all right? I asked, almost stumbling on the word.

Healthy and happy, she said. As far as one can tell.

She lifted her hands up slightly, as though playing piano, held them there for a second, then pulled my T-shirt back down, took the gloves off and stood up.

I sat up and inspected the skin of my hands. Four small bloody marks on each palm. I tried to hide them from her but she took disinfectant and cotton wool and dressings and cleaned the wounds, bandaged up my palms lightly, and then she held each finger individually as she clipped my nails. She gave me a nightgown of her own. Pink, sprigged with the buds of white flowers. She left a map on my bed. Do it right, if you're going to do it, she had written on its front page. The shape of our country seemed sharper than I remembered from school, different even, with many more roads. Before I went to sleep I drew a route. It was just a line meandering upwards on the smaller roads, essentially meaningless, but it calmed me. Back roads, uncharted territory. One step at a time.

In the night I walked out of the door and down the road into a field of sunflowers. They were taller than me. The dirt was loose. In the dark their faces were not cheerful. I held on to their stems. In the centre of the field, a dark animal with glowing eyes. It grew bigger, and then smaller. It grew human-shaped, small, like a child or a teenager. I ran back to bed in the nightgown and slept for a long time.

The cats woke me, leaping on to the bed like demons. They wanted to suck out my breath, the way that cats always do. I batted them away. The natural world was hostile. The animals saw what the humans didn't want to see but I was different now, and I could see it too. The old woman was taking her coffee in a narrow garden out the back. I did not disturb her, did not want her advice or her warnings, so I just left her some money on top of the guestbook and walked outside. It was early morning, wet and sharp, and I drove one-handed, the other hand on my bump, and I was alive, I was alive, it was irrefutable. There was a clarity that lived within me, and this clarity came with every breath.

7

In a service station I filled a can with petrol and then ordered a hot dog with crisped onions from a man with a white hat pulled over his sweating hair. He barely acknowledged me. I was sweating too, gleaming brightly as a person in fever. I ate the hot dog in the car, feral, in a dark spot of shade so that nobody could see me, but afterwards I had to throw it up, on my knees despite the sodden rest-stop tiles. My jeans were filthy. The high wheeze of the fan unit was like a mosquito, an auditory protest.

Somebody came in and I pulled my knees up to my chest, watched the shoes pace the length of the room then retract, choosing the stall furthest away from me. I heard them making a noise that could be crying, blowing their nose, the toilet flushing. Please do it elsewhere, I wanted to tell them with the greatest compassion I could muster. I had to be sick again, quietly. My body was in revolt. When the person left I rinsed my mouth with the tap water and spat pinkly into the bowl, washed my hands three times, splashed water on myself. I knew that I had to go, that I always had to be going.

There was a middle-aged woman on the till of the gift shop; I saw her as I passed, folding T-shirts into slippery plastic bags. Her locket was just visible under her T-shirt. I wanted her to open it, wanted to press my pistol to her head and see what she would do, what she would reveal. These violent urges had been taking me by surprise for weeks now and they were not distressing in the way I would have expected them to be. Perhaps this was what motherhood did to you, why it was not suitable for every woman to go into. I imagined the metal, hot in my hand, and my other hand twisting in her hair.

I drove until dark fell, and then some more. My headlights snagged on a person pushed into a hedge. Whoever it was flung their arm across their face and I saw they were dirty, scratched. It was a young girl, I realized, and I stopped the car. She remained motionless, so I opened the door of the driver's side.

Where are you going? Can I give you a lift? I asked.

She looked at me but didn't answer, eyes swollen, as if she had been crying. I pulled my loose shirt over my stomach, though she wasn't going to do anything. She did not resemble me or my younger self in the slightest, but I looked for myself in her and found it anyway. It was in the dark marks on her sweater and shorts that could have been blood. It was in her hair, unbrushed, matted in places.

I'm looking for a city, she said, finally. I glanced at the locket around her neck, untarnished, knew how the weight of it would remain a foreign object for some time.

I'm going the opposite way, I said.

Can you just drive me for a bit? she pleaded. Just a bit?

Wait, wait, I said. Don't move. I'm thinking.

I went to the boot of the car, stuffed everything into my backpack, strapped the sleeping bag to its side. She watched me as I emptied the car, leaving just some food and the old map. When I went up to her and opened my hand she flinched, but I presented her with the keys.

You stay quiet and stick to back roads, I told her as I strapped the pack to my back, ungainly. Gather rainwater. Do you know how to drive a car?

Yes, she said. My father taught me.

Do you know how to skin a rabbit? I asked.

Yes, she said.

Down the stomach and open it up; spread the ribs and tip the insides on the ground, I said, just in case.

I knew how they would steam in the air; how she would stay up all night next to them, rank copper scent in her nostrils. Owls overhead, bats. The dripping of rain enough to make you prick your ears, run as far as you could.

I know, she repeated. Thank you.

Her ankles were a mess from moving through the undergrowth, calves swollen with bites. My heart pulled and released. Good luck, I told her, walking across the road. She stood there, disbelieving.

Don't just watch me, I called back to her. You have to drive.

I waited until she pulled out, unsteady, and into the road. If she sat up straight and tied her hair back she could pass for an adult. She could pick up other girls on the way. She could find safety. And yet part of me thought *Why should she have it easy when I did not?* and another part was horrified at this thought, because the blood showed it had not been easy, the locket showed it was not going to be easy whatever she did. We were so careless with our girls. Defence was a learned behaviour. I had learned it. I was passing it on. My hand stroked the pistol in the deep pocket of my denim jacket.

When a car passed me I folded over into the grassy ditch. My backpack dug into my shoulders. I felt strangely free without the car. Now there was no shell from the world. Now there was just me.

8

I walked through the night. Without Doctor A's guidance, I spoke to rocks. I spoke to dirt. I climbed into a field and sat in the long grass and spoke to the sky as the sun rose. I spoke to the palm of my hand, pressed right up close so there was only the hot tickle of my breath and my own words, reflected back at me.

How are you feeling, how are you feeling? I said to myself. What is your mind doing?

My heartburn was bad and I was longing to push my nose into wet, newly cut grass. Foods I had hated I thought of suddenly with passion, and foods I had liked I now despised. It was galling, to be so tricked about everything.

I camped in the field, though I was not supposed to be there. I would sleep through the day and move at night, I decided. I would get better at this. The field was full of huge brown cows, milling around the far end with looks of great alarm. I picked up small rocks to throw at them but was too afraid of provoking a stampede, too tired to stay awake, so I let them be.

And then night-time, before I knew it. Pooling dark inside the canvas. I lay on the hard ground listening to the heavy creatures around me.

When I unzipped the tent, the air and grass were wet. In the distance, by moonlight, I could see mountains still. When I breathed deeply my lungs felt new, and this newness soaked into the rest of me. It was possible that every time I saw a mountain, even my thousandth mountain, I would be possessed by an involuntary gratefulness. It was enough to see it. To remember. With slow movements I packed up my things. The cows were doleful. They did not want to crush me to death after all. I touched one of them on the head, its soft ear. Goodbye, I said.

Up the road there was a bus stop. I waited there for some time in the dark. One large bus passed but did not stop. The people on their own journeys, looking out of the windows, illuminated by reading lights above their heads like spotlights.

Another bus came soon enough. It too was large, with high, plush seats that were worn and smelled of old sweat. North, the driver said when I asked the destination, which was good enough for me. An old man was sitting near the back so I sat in the middle, where it was darkest. I didn't want to be near anyone.

Soon the old man came and talked to me anyway, like I knew he would. He peered over the seat. I leaned against the window, away from him. My cheek wet on dirty glass, pretending to be asleep.

You're not sleeping, he said. He pressed one hand against the window behind me.

My eyes closed, then opened. There were no lights to be seen, just countryside. A car overtook us, graceful as a deer.

Don't be rude, he said.

I'm tired, I said. It's late.

Where are you going, he said. He smelled faintly, sweetly, of piss. In the darkness of the bus I could only really see the shadow of him behind me. I shifted slightly.

I'm going to meet my husband, I said.

He laughed. Husband, sure, he said.

R. He's an emissary, I improvised. I was in love with my made-up husband who could keep me safe. This tall and kind man trailing me across the country, saying *come back to me*, saying *let's be a family*. Always I had taken pride in being alone and now all this, the soggy desire to be boxed in a house with people I was bound to. I tried to own this new desire the way I had owned others, but it was shameful to me.

You wouldn't be on this bus if you had a husband, he said. He tapped the pack with his hand. I know what you've got in here.

I'm sleeping now, I said.

I'll keep your secret if you do something nice for me, he said. His hand moved to his belt buckle. I tried to evaluate the strength of my body versus his as he took a long drink from a bottle in a brown paper bag. Brandy? he asked, but I shook my head.

Come on, he said, we don't have all day. He fumbled with his zip; I heard the sound of it giving way, sensed the outline of what he held. I didn't need to see it. He made a cooing noise, like a dove felled. I wanted to make a hard object from the flat of my hand and push it upwards into his nose, the way I had learned to break a man's face, but I didn't have it in me. I stood up and took my pack, walked down the aisle of the lurching bus to a seat nearer the driver. The man shouted, Frigid blue bitch! and then fell silent, otherwise occupied.

I stood by the driver. Let me off, I said. I don't care where, just let me off.

You want to get off here, in the dark? The driver kept his eyes on the road. Two long hard beams of light running smoothly over tarmac.

What did my friend do that was so bad? So bad that you want to be left here in the middle of nowhere?

I could tell from the way the man was hunched over that he was still holding himself, even from several seats away. I was glad I couldn't see it. Squirming, too-alive flesh. A fish or a plucked bird. Not R stretched out on the bed of the love motel, long and beautiful even under artificial light, my eyes and my hands, the taste of the beer on my lips. Everything good could be made ugly, it was inescapable.

Let me off, I said. I'm not kidding.

On your head be it, the driver said. He pulled over to a lay-by, idled the engine. Get out then if you're going to get out, he said. He started to move the bus before I had made it off and I jumped on to the gravel, skidding, scraping the flesh from my knee. The two men were laughing at me, I could hear the laughing even with the doors closing. Go fuck yourselves, I shouted as the bus pulled away, which was not very brave of me because there was no way they could hear, no way they would care if they did.

I kept walking. The backpack hurt my shoulders and in the dark there was the illusion of going nowhere, which might not have even been an illusion, but all I could do was put one foot after the other and see what happened. As I walked, I realized I was lonely. I wanted to tell someone about the violence bubbling under my skin, and to hear another person's private desires in return, to find communion in that.

To swim together in the depths of wanting, moving out from the land's edge to somewhere else.

And I thought of the baby, doing their own kind of swimming. My body was the only ocean they had ever known. I felt so protective when I thought about this that I could almost fall over. I wanted to curl my body into a soft sack of flesh and bury myself deep in order to keep safe for them. I wanted to emerge from the earth and know I had ferried them, perfectly, to the shore.

9

The sun was high in the sky by the time I reached the next town. I walked through the houses of the outskirts until the streets became small and winding, houses pressed close to each other, and then tasteful shops with ceramics in the window, bakeries, little bars with the shutters still down. At the heart of it I came to a large freshwater lake. I took my shoes off and walked across the lake's beach, made up of small white pebbles, until I reached the icy water. I let it come up to my knees. It was perfectly still. The water was slate grey. The water was a kind of blue. I knew that blue was a relatively new concept in terms of colour, that for a long time we had not recognized or seen it, that colour sense was a gradual unveiling, and that being pregnant felt like that. There had been something in the world that my eyes had not picked up on, and now it was everywhere. I didn't even want to see it, didn't want my perception to have been so altered. I didn't want to know that everything was trying to kill me. Strange, to be so truly vulnerable.

This was the kind of place where mothers lived, where white-ticket women lived. They were somewhere nearby. I saw pairs of them walking together with their arms linked, no babies, net shopping bags filled with fruits and vegetables. In a shop I picked up a black maternity dress with yellow spots and a white leotard for a baby. Here, perhaps I could be who I wanted to be. I didn't have to be a woman hounded off buses, a woman tricked into bathrooms, a drinker, a slut, a piece of shit. My hands skimmed over the shrunken vests, the socks like egg warmers or knitted thimbles, striped hats. I would not be sent away like I had been in the city, I would refuse it.

Don't you want to try it on? the woman at the counter asked. Her hair was done up in a complicated braid, her cheeks very pink. No, I said. She slipped them into a paper bag for me and I left at once, walking as quickly as I could. I looked around for emissaries, stretching their legs on a lunchtime walk or reading the newspaper at a table outside.

In a café up a side street a safe distance away, I ordered a pot of tea and sat outside, sunglasses on, pretending to read the newspaper. The news was all bad. The ashtray was full. The kind waitress came to empty it and to bring me my tea. Are you on holiday? she asked. I nodded. Oh, you've come to the right place, there is no place more beautiful than here, she told me, she was glowing with certainty, she didn't even seem to notice my silence or the bad way I smelled or my jeans still rolled up and wet from the lake. I was performing motherhood the way I had performed adulthood, all those years ago. I was acting like it was something I deserved and could do.

It didn't take long before I saw a father with one of the large prams, the design slightly different here to the ones I saw in the city. He seemed harassed, in a rush. I tried to make myself invisible. The waitress ran outside and hailed him, pressed an offering of a small cake into his hand and then looked into the pram. Oh hello, beautiful, she said to the baby. Oh, aren't you a lovely one.

I went prowling for other fathers, for as many as I could find. They slipped around corners, moved through the aisles of shops. Some were tall and some were short, some were handsome and others less so, but all had the pram and all were accosted, by men and women, wherever they went, though not with the same energy as in the city, where families were rarer to see. I tried to hear the sound of the babies. I could not picture my own father pushing around a pram, but I knew that he must have. I wondered what kind of father R would make one day, if he would ever be one, if he would take the gifts reluctantly or hold the baby up for everyone to see with such pride that it was like he thought nobody had ever seen one before.

One of the fathers had red hair and a beard. He reminded me of Doctor A; for a second I thought it was him. I found a coin in my purse and dropped it in his bag. Thank you, he said. Can I? I asked, conscious of my sweat, my unwashed hair. He pulled back the blanket a little reluctantly. The baby was asleep, swaddled like something you needed to unpeel. I wished to kiss her face but that would cross a line. Instead I touched her on the cheek, one finger. It was hard not to cry but I managed it.

She's really beautiful, I said. I smiled in what I hoped was a winning fashion, eyes wide, but I did not register to him beyond a mouth, a set of teeth. He was a father now, overheated and stressed out, and so by definition he could not be tempted. Thanks, he said, already looking to where he needed to go.

I let them move onwards, waited before following a safe distance behind. It was difficult because every few minutes the father was required to stop so that the baby could be looked at, and it was harder to hide than it would have been in the city. All the buildings were painted shades of white, and some of them had ivy or honeysuckle dripping down.

The father walked faster. He reached the edge of the town and then started on a pavement that led to the suburbs. It was riskier to follow him here; I lost my nerve, let myself fall back further, until the shape of him was tiny in the distance, the bag on his shoulder now full of coins and cakes and other offerings. I thought about what it would be like to pull him to the ground and press my body to his. I would seduce all the fathers and pummel them with my fists, and they would like it. I would crawl into the homes of the white-ticket women and overturn the beds where they and their babies lay, to be their nightmares, if I could not be them. I was vengeful and wanted it all.

The baby, my own bad baby come from badness, was sucking the marrow from my bones. I pitched my tent on a patch of hard ground surrounded by trees, and there I slept away the ragged, compromised hours of the afternoon. In my dreams I saw the woman called Marisol, walking through fields of sunflowers, lying down next to me on the gravel, so real that I expected her to be there when I awoke, but she was not there, and my body was covered in thousands of tiny bruises where I had moved around on the ground, my injured knee was throbbing, and I understood in a way that felt new that my skin was nothing but a membrane holding in organic matter, that I could spill everywhere like a glass of water if anything wounded me.

10

The clean town and daylight weren't for me. I needed neglected roads, patches of earth ripe with decay and mud where I could pitch my tent. In a roadside bar, between buses, I nursed beer mixed with lemonade and threw darts, practising my aim. I watched men come in and sit alone, couples unsteady on their feet, dancing with hands at waists, shoulders, faces. They were my favourite, they had eyes only for each other. It would have been easy to resent them for it, but one weak drink in and I became benevolent, like an angel, deciding to forgive them their happiness.

I remembered comfort in bodies – comfort in my own and others'. Desire was a leveller. It put us on the same plane. Allowed forgetting and forgiveness. Into my beer I reminisced like an old man about mouth after mouth, about tucking the hair of a woman whose name I didn't remember behind her ear so she could hear me better as I spoke into it, about pressing my shoulder into the arm of a man whose name I didn't remember either and him not pulling away, the thrill of his complicity.

You are made for this life and not the other, Doctor A had said to me once. Think about all the joy you let run through your fingers like it is nothing. The problem with you is that you don't take advantage of your freedom in the way that you should. I mean, you could do anything. He paused. Almost anything.

I believed, sometimes, that he had a point.

As the dawn came up I made myself a bed with my sleeping bag among the grass and the leaves, sheltered and well away from the road, but without the tent. I wanted to remember what it had been like the first time. I wanted to be a natural part of the landscape. Fatigue dragged at me. Summer had arrived, I realized. I fell asleep in sunlight and woke up in it, still safe. I lay there and listened to the chirruping of insects, birds.

Another bar that night. A man with tattooed wrists, feathering cards out on to wet red leather. Ace of diamonds. Queen of hearts. He smiled a gap-toothed grin. I rested my face on my interlaced hands, looked up adoringly, but when he was in the bathroom I left.

I have blindly obeyed you, I told my body. I have followed you wherever you want to take me. Now what?

Now, I don't know, my body said back. Just wait.

In the next bar, the crowd was more talkative, people tried to engage me in earnest, and so I just removed myself from the situation. I walked until it became light and then I slept on the ground and then I walked some more, and I thought I could live my life like this for a while at least, I didn't really need much more – I could just go, I could be free. Except that, in a new way, I would never be free again. The terse thrill of remembering this, for it did not feel like being trapped in the way that my old freedom had.

As I walked I couldn't help but think, *Nothing that bad has happened to you yet*. Maybe it was all a lie. Maybe I had got away with it, from it, maybe they had realized there were bigger things to concern themselves with. In the parking area of a roadside restaurant I pulled stale bread from the large bins outside, and I remembered that it could feel delicious to rip at food that way, in the clear air, all teeth and hands. When I slept I kept my knife in my hand; I was no longer drowsy on waking, but alert. I was remembering.

Perhaps the run of luck made me too confident. I know that when I passed a hotel as I walked one night in particular dark, my back killing me, my feet took me up the path towards it before I could check myself. *What's the harm.* The woman on the desk looked me up and down and I did the same to her, defensively: the cheap red suit with puffed sleeves, her yellow hair teased and then brushed down again. The glint of her locket chain where it slunk invitingly around her neck. Sweat ran down inside my T-shirt. I knew without looking that my feet were bloody inside my shoes.

Maybe you want to be caught, I said to myself as I followed her up the stairwell. Maybe Doctor A has always been right. Despite myself, there was a pang when I thought about him. I was still unused to living without the weight of his instruction. It would have been good to be told how to feel. To be translated. The bed had a slippery pale green bedspread, cold satin. It was like lying in water. I pushed it off the bed and among the sheets I started writing Doctor A a letter using the hotel's stationery set that started *In some ways I have loved you more deeply than anyone*, but I caught myself in time and ripped, flushed it down the toilet in shreds, horrified at what my heart was capable of, its deceitful electricity. In the minibar there were whisky miniatures. Medicinal, I told myself, unscrewing the top of one with my teeth and spitting the lid across the room. The liquid burned in my mouth. There was a telephone on the bedside table. I picked it up and dialled R's number.

Hello, I said. I tugged on the spiralled cord that transmitted my words to his. My breath reflected back at myself.

Who is this? he asked.

Who do you want it to be? I asked.

I could hear a woman in the background. She asked, Who's that?

I don't know what you want, he said.

I just want you to put the phone down on the side and go about your evening so I can hear what you're doing, I said. Will you do that for me?

There was definitely a woman. R, who is it? she said.

Who's that? I asked.

He breathed hard.

She sounds nice. I bet she's a white-ticket, I said, and then I punched the wall, lightly, just thinking about it, just knowing that I was right, that the experience of me would have driven him into the arms of someone docile and warm.

I refuse to discuss that with you, he said. What was that noise?

Nothing, I said, examining my knuckles, which were not even grazed.

Look, he said. I don't know what you want from me. I don't know what you want me to say.

I want you to say that you love me, I said. I want you to come and rescue me and be a family with me and the baby past the border. I think it might be possible, but only if you come now.

He hissed very lightly through his teeth as if in anger or great despair, I couldn't tell, that was the difficulty of the telephone, but really either reaction was fine with me. Prank caller, he said to the woman on his end of the phone, then hung up. I rang back but nobody answered.

I called Doctor A next, of course. It was quite late so I used his personal phone number, emergencies only. He didn't ask where I was or how I was.

Calla, he said. It's very late.

I need to hear you say something to me, something grounding, I said.

Are you in an emergency? he said.

I don't know — not yet, maybe, I said. But I might be in one soon.

That's a little manipulative, don't you think? he said.

I hate that word, I said.

Only when it's applied to you, he said. I'm afraid I can't help you tonight. I maybe can't help you ever again. Sleep well, Calla.

Wasted opportunity. I felt glad I hadn't finished the letter after all. My fingers pressed at random on the keypad. A woman answered. I could hear her smoking.

Hello? she asked. Hello, hello, hello?

Is anyone out there? I asked. I just want to speak to someone.

What are you looking for? she asked.

Anything, all of it, I said. Are you lonely?

She laughed sharply and hung up.

I rang R again but there was no answer. So I threw the telephone against the wall but it did not break, it was an old instrument made of sterner stuff. There was not even a mark left on the plaster.

I I

There was no bath so I sat inside the shower and wept. The small soap was the colour of cheese, the size of a large coin. I pressed it between my palms. I dug my nails into it.

The first hotel I had ever seen in my life was a hotel on my journey into the city. I had sat down gingerly on top of clean sheets at the far end of a large bed. My legs were ripped up from all the brambles that year. You can take a shower and lock the door if you want, the man who had found me walking on the side of the road had said.

The man was youngish, tall and handsome, otherwise I would not have got into the car. I was comforted by the fact that he looked like he could be a minor film star, and the memory of the white-ticket girl in her own car, the tinted windows, the emissary taking her somewhere. Perhaps this was the car for me, the car I had always been supposed to take but had somehow missed, all part of the test. In the car I had noticed his hands, the way they wouldn't stop moving on the steering wheel. Perhaps I was wrong. Perhaps I was going to be murdered. Both possibilities refracted out. He had given me a stick of mauve chewing gum and a cigarette and allowed me to pick the station on the radio.

I had stepped out of that first hotel shower and slipped my locket back on while I was still wet. I put on the clean bathrobe from the back of the door. The waterproof coat that I had stolen from a service station weeks ago was in the other room, draped on a chair. Miniature comb. Toothpicks. Cotton buds. I brushed my teeth for a long time.

The man had been sitting on the bed when I got out, leaning back against all the pillows and watching the television. He had unbuttoned the collar of his white shirt and hung up his black suede jacket in the wardrobe. My turn, he said, smiling a small smile. He went into the bathroom and shut the door but did not lock it. I moved through the channels on the television. I looked at the room service menu.

You're tall for your age, he said when he came back in, wet-haired, towel around his waist. I averted my eyes. It wasn't like I had never imagined a scenario similar, but in my fantasies there had been standing under the moon beforehand, with the stars pointed out to me. Perhaps, also, a rose in a long white box. Here, there were no stars. There was a flower découpage on the wall. An old map of the area, the lake picked out in aquamarine.

He walked towards me and asked if he could look at the locket. I said yes. He knelt in front of me, opened it, saw the blue, closed it again. He brushed a lock of wet hair from my cheek. Are you hungry? he asked and I nodded; I was starving. He picked up the phone and ordered two cheeseburgers. They came to the door of the hotel room smoothly, within minutes. Stay back, he said to me before he answered the door, still just in the towel. We ate the food on the floor. White wine spritzer for me, beer for him.

Would I mind lying on the bed, he asked me after, almost apologetically. He unwrapped the robe. I experimented with kissing him whenever his mouth was near mine, too jerkily, like a bird trying to eat. Then I looked away from him and towards the flocked ceiling instead, embarrassed by myself, embarrassed for him. I'll drive you

137

where you need to go, he said afterwards, and he did, in the morning, after I had slept in that first hotel bed. The first time my body had got me somewhere. I felt a tiredness so total that I woke only when the man touched my locket in the morning – gently, but still I felt it.

In the car we did not talk. We had both showered again and his hair was still damp, parted neatly. In the shower I had folded over and touched my toes, had hung there and let gravity work on me until I felt I would fall. He was not a minor film star, after all. I tried to decide whether I could be in love with him. He gave me a crisp note, a big one. Be safe, he said, before driving off. We were in a town near the city. After he left I bought a litre of orange juice and a new dress, stood outside in a patch of sunlight and chugged half the juice right down in one go. In the bathroom of a café I changed into the dress, peach cotton, and then I went out and sat down and asked for a cup of coffee and the paper.

It was in that dress that I walked into the city. He told me I couldn't enter in someone else's car. It had to be on foot. I have sisters, he had said. I could still smell the hotel smell on me. The small shampoo, doll-like in my wet hand that morning as I soaped my hair once, twice. You can take them all, he had said to me, and when we walked past the reception my heart had kicked, I thought they would see I was a thief, the miniature body lotions and conditioners in my rucksack knocking against each other, but nobody stopped me.

All the worse things that I knew I would do in the future stretched out ahead of me, and in a way they were possibilities that possessed their own depraved charm. They showed me I was capable. I didn't feel sad or ashamed or used. In my own way, in a way that would become familiar to me soon enough, I felt good.

12

I left the telephone where it was, showered, put on the dark red lipstick and walked out of my room, to the lift. The carpet was thick and soft against my bare feet, peachy-brown. No time to put my shoes on. No time to wait for the lift; I walked down the stairwell. Flickering cold light. The bar in the hotel was mostly empty. I ordered a whisky and sat at a table in the corner, curling my bare feet under myself. I flipped a coaster back and forth, a tic learned from R. The coaster advertised iron-enriched beer. I tore it, a little, just because I could. My teeth felt too big for my mouth, and hard. I was the only woman. Pick a man, any man, I said to myself. Do it. I stared at a short man with dark hair sitting up at the bar on a stool. The bar was mint green and fake marble, the seats vinyl. I did not think he looked like an emissary, but then, who could tell. I had been wrong about so many things and I would keep being wrong. He kept turning to look at me and eventually came over.

Where are your shoes? he asked. I smiled.

I ate them, I said.

The man motioned to the barman, who nodded and took two glasses down from a shelf. I watched him as he poured things. He was making martinis. He brought them over on a round copper tray. Paper-thin lemon. The glasses were very cold. It was the most delicious thing I had ever tasted.

What brings you here? the man asked.

Everything, I said, taking a sip. *Bad mother, bad mother.*

You're not very forthcoming. You don't talk very much, he said. You're not giving me anything to work with.

Well, I don't have that much to say, I said.

Maybe you're the kind of person who only speaks when they have something to tell, he said. Or maybe you're into other things, rather than talking.

I think you might be right, I said. About the other things.

Don't you want to know about me? he asked.

No, not really, I said, and he laughed. The laugh seemed charmed by my rudeness, not angry. I took another mouthful of my drink. Somewhere in the background a woman was singing to an orchestra. The music came out of a speaker above our table. I looked up from under my eyelashes, I let him see the clean line of my throat.

But what happened to your shoes, really? he said.

I'll let you in on a secret, I said, leaning in. I've never worn a pair of shoes in my life. I've always just walked around in my bare feet. My skin is unnaturally strong. I've never needed them.

So you're a medical miracle? he said.

That's right, I said. At my birth the doctor proclaimed it an unprecedented event. He carried me around the hospital personally so that everyone could see me.

Can I see these magical feet? he asked.

I swung them into his soft-trousered lap. Certainly, I said. Knock yourself out.

The barman watched us from where he stood, as if keeping tabs.

My story held up – they did indeed seem like the feet of somebody who had never worn shoes. My toes were jewelled with calluses, red and swollen, though at least they weren't bleeding any more. I could see now that two of my smaller toenails had dropped off, the way I had experienced previously after six months of running in too-small trainers without caring. The man caressed them anyway, as if there were nothing wrong. It made me feel sick to see him touching me like that, holding those ugly pieces of me with such reverence. It made me feel murderous, like I could crush him like an insect and he would thank me for it. I pulled my feet away but then leaned over to kiss him instead.

Come to my room, he said. We walked out of the bar together. I was shaking. The lift, as it turned out, was broken, so we walked. In the dark stairwell he pressed me up against the badly painted wall. The sound of the lift trying and failing to move came through. Everything smelled of bleach. I batted his hands away from my locket and they moved instead to my jeans. I tensed as they skimmed over my stomach, my waist.

Lie down on the floor, I told him.

Here? he asked, panting.

Yes, here, I said. Lie down and close your eyes and pretend to be dead.

He lay down on the carpet and closed his eyes. I straddled him and undid his belt buckle. The thin skin of his eyelids twitched. Underneath the stubble his skin was red, the veins and blood were alive. His lips twitched in a smile.

You're not pretending hard enough, I said.

I wanted to be powerful, I wanted the violence under my skin to come back and tell me what to do, to direct me. I wanted to fuck and to be fucked until I was outside of my own head, I wanted a barrel of alcohol, I wanted mind-altering drugs, I wanted to slit his throat – but it was all gone into another world.

I got off him. He sat up and laughed, not maliciously. He took me to his room. It was better than mine. We have to turn off all the lights, I said. I was going to go through with it. Turn off the lights, I said again, and finally he did.

On the bed I cried, silently, because he couldn't see me. Because nothing was going to make me feel better, nothing was going to be enough. I cried for the absence of women I had seen on the road, for having to do this alone. I cried because R didn't want to have the baby with me and because Doctor A was my enemy and he wasn't going to save or fix me.

Please don't cry, the man said, gently. Not with your beautiful feet. Your miracle body.

I knelt in the dark and waited. Palms on satin. Which angle would the man come from, what would he do to me first, what did he want me to do. My brain floated out like a balloon. Stay present, I told myself, connection is connection. His hand was soft on the small of my back. His hands were not unkind. We were two lost bodies speaking the same, or a similar, language. Still, I wanted another martini. I wanted a dozen people in the room, watching and participating. I wasn't sure if I would come but I did, almost instantly, despite the shame, or maybe because of it. I thought about Doctor A as it happened, about the clinical disgust he would feel if he could see me now. I started to cry again and didn't care if the man saw or felt.

I'm going, I said, crawling off the edge of the bed and on to the floor. I felt around for my clothes and pulled them on.

Don't go, don't go, he said, turning on the lights. We've just got started.

No, I said, pushing past him, we're done, thank you for the drink.

He held on to my arm and took a long blink, gathering patience. When he opened his eyes they were hard. I've had enough of your bullshit, he said. I've been good to you and I don't deserve to be treated like this.

He raised his hand and hit me in the face full on, without hesitating, a weak punch. The pain kaleidoscoped me out of myself and then back in, but I'd felt worse and I told him so – I looked him in the eye and said, That didn't even hurt, the blood trickling hot on my top lip, gathering then releasing into my mouth. It tasted good – nourishing, reassuring, like my own unwashed scent in the mornings. All at once my focus was sharp. I didn't care enough about myself but I cared about the baby. I opened the door and started running.

Where are you going? I heard him shout. He sounded bereft. Come back, come back!

I leapt, I flew through the air, I found the stairs, I found my floor, I did not stop, I opened my door in one go and slammed it behind me. I sat on the floor and listened to the sound of him roaming around like a bull.

Where are you? he was bellowing. Where did you go?

Even I didn't really know.

Is it out of your system now? I asked myself, crawling away from the door on my hands and knees. Are you done?

Only white in the space between my thoughts. A split of light in the darkness, under the door. It felt good to be low to the ground.

He moved further away but I could still hear him. *Someone must shut him up*, I thought, very carefully not thinking about what would happen if no one did, and eventually there was silence. Maybe I was a slut, maybe I had lured him under false pretences, but that was acceptable, that was not unforgivable the way that being pregnant was. I was bleeding a little, inside my mouth. I let pink saliva spool down on to the carpet, and then on to the sheets. I didn't take the red lipstick off and the blood got everywhere, all over the nice expensive-feeling bedspread, like I had ripped something apart.

13

It was coming into dawn and I knew I had to go. Time was spiralling away from me. As I walked down the corridors of the hotel I sensed the leering faces of people behind the doors, people taking a break from their own degradations to peer through the peepholes and watch my steps.

I hesitated at the base of the stairs, reluctant to go past the reception desk in case the man was there, though nobody was around so early. Instead I ducked through back corridors until I came to a fire door and pushed my way into crisp air, a slight sweet rotting smell from hotel bins piled high. A fox worrying at a plastic bag ran away. I climbed over a low fence into somebody's garden, and then another, until I reached the road again. The morning was clear and bright and I tried to take joy in it, whatever good feeling I could manage, but it didn't work. My lip hurt and tasted of metal. My body wanted R's arms around it. The smell of his neck. It was all muscle memory, sentimentality for something that had never really existed. I reminded myself of that, though the truth stung.

The next bus was empty except for an old woman and another man, this one much younger, slouching at the back. I kept away from them both but of course the man moved to find me, like before, swaying as he came down the aisle of the bus. I was burning up. Adrenaline zipped at the surface of my skin.

Hello, what's your name? he asked. He smiled widely and beautifully. One of his canine teeth was missing.

I don't have a name, I said, this time.

What happened to your face? he asked.

I touched my split lip. It's always been like this, I said.

He smiled beatifically and rummaged in a hessian tote bag. He handed me a square of violet paper. Not a blue ticket. I held it in the palm of my hand.

I can't eat this, I said.

I've had three already, he said to me, which explained his woozy pupils, his wet face. It's the only way to travel by bus, he said, and laughed like a hyena. He was younger than I had first thought, late teens perhaps. With his gapped mouth he looked like a child over-grown, three feet taller than he should be.

Tell me what you see, I asked him.

He pointed at the lurid bus seat in front of him. The roots are coming out, he said. The flowers are all in the meadow and they are reaching to the sky. Dancing around as happy as you like.

He shuffled to the window and pressed his face to the glass. And look, he said. Outside there is the universe, and all the other cars are flying. They're like birds above us.

When he pulled his face away he left a gentle smear on the glass from his sweating cheek.

I looked out of the window on my side. I wanted to see what he could see, it sounded better than my world, but I was not going to take the tab – even I knew that a mother would not do that. A white-ticket would have already got off the bus.

Your head is a sunflower, he said. It's okay, he reassured me. You can still be alive. It suits you.

He stretched out his legs and stared at his feet for a while. He was wearing filthy, red-toed white trainers. I watched his face move through fear and acceptance and back to the beautiful smile, before he turned to me again.

Let's play rock, paper, scissors, he said, but we couldn't get very far because he kept stopping to stare at his hands and mine.

Where are you going? I asked as he held my wrist and examined my fingers. He brought them right up to his face, taking in every whorl and grain of dirt.

Home, he said. Home!

But where is that? I asked.

Close by, he said.

He fell asleep, his cheeks flushed. He was somebody's son. Somebody out there had kept him safe. Outside it was raining now, the water sluicing down the windows. Our journeys were different but intersecting briefly. I wished him all good things. I wished to keep somebody safe too.

14

In the service station we dispersed into the sparse crowd. It wasn't busy that time of day. I kept my eyes very open, made my way to the bathroom and sat in a stall, breathed. A light sigh came from the one next to me. I watched the shadows cast by their feet as they moved. The stall felt safe, I didn't want to leave it and go back into the world. I wanted only marbled white formica, lino wearing at the edges, a confined and clean space.

When I worked up the strength to leave the stall, there was a woman with long black hair washing her hands in a basin. She had a methodical way of washing – soaping over her palms, up over her wrists, down again as if brushing off something. Rinse and then lather again. I could have watched her all day. I took a place at the basin next to hers and attempted her thoroughness. Our eyes met in the mirror and I forgot about washing my hands. Marisol, I said. There was a smudge of dirt at her temple. Her face registered a brief but intense surprise. She rinsed her hands one last time and then bent over the sink and washed her face gracefully.

You remembered my name, she said.

Are you following me? I asked. I tried to look threatening but it didn't land.

I should ask you the same thing, she said. Who would follow you? You don't even have the right map.

I have one now, I said.

She smiled at me. Well done, well done, a gold star for you.

We went together to the wet rooms without discussing it. Coins into the turnstile, we took off our clothes and stepped under the jets of water, bodies separated by a thin laminate partition. The proximity made me feel giddy. We didn't speak. Water pooled from her side into mine and I bent down to touch it, I had the wild idea that I wanted to drink it. And then I thought, *Oh, I recognize this*, and it was funny to feel something other than fear, desperation, to know that other feelings were still possible. I leaned against the partition and imagined her body doing the same. Arm to arm, leg to leg.

When I brushed my teeth in the shower, too vigorously, and I spat on to the floor, there was blood in the foam and the terrible sensation of something loose in my mouth – gravel, dirt, bone. My hands in my own mouth, panicked. My tooth, I called to Marisol. Something's wrong.

We dressed and met outside the cubicles. Wet-haired, barefoot, she peered into my mouth. That needs to come out, she said. Want me to get it now? I can pull it out. It'll hurt but only for a little. I love pulling out teeth.

No, I said. I pulled tissue paper from the dispenser and held it to my mouth to stem the bleeding.

It's normal, she said. It's the new normal. The baby takes a tooth. Did nobody ever tell you?

Nobody told me anything, I said, the paper slowly growing wet with my own blood. Nobody fucking told me a thing! And I was suddenly so angry about it.

Look, she said, baring her own gums, gapped and pink at the back.

We left the wet rooms and emerged into an arcade area, electronic games pinging and flashing. I leaned against the brightest one, worrying at the tooth with my tongue. I'm going to miss my bus, I said as she pushed coins into a machine and pulled the lever. It's probably already gone.

Stay with me, she said, her face lit red and yellow, eyes trained on the pictures spinning around.

Aren't you with someone else already? I asked, trying to remain casual.

Oh, she went off not long after we met, she said. We had different ideas. Perhaps the same will be true for us. But two minds are always better than one.

All right, I said, after thinking about it for a few seconds.

You should have hesitated longer, she said. I could still kill you.

I can protect myself, I said.

She moved suddenly, pressed me up against the wall with one hand twisted behind my back. I felt not panic but excitement, my heart jumping up a notch. Prove it, she said.

Nobody else could see us at that angle. Her body pressed to my back.

Her mouth felt close to my neck, her breath hot on my skin. I couldn't see if she held a knife. I kicked backwards instinctively, wrenched my arm away and took hold of my own knife, spun around to face her. She was flushed, rubbing her shin where my foot had made contact, her eye on my knife where it trembled in the air. The noise of people walking past just a few metres away, carrying food, the arcade machines singing out.

All right, she said. Consider me convinced.

My breath was hard and I was warm everywhere. The machine nearest us showered coins. Marisol scooped them into her hands, her pockets, with small but visible delight.

Let's go then, she said. She moved decisively out towards the car park, and did not look back to see if I would follow.

15

Marisol was better at survival than I was. She had pitched her first tent in a field and left it there within the crucial starting hours, buying a new one, a khaki one that blended in. She had driven the first car into a lake and swum to the surface some way away, hoping they were watching and would presume her dead. She had done a swap, a trade, for the second, but she didn't elaborate.

You need to let yourself remember how you did it before, she said to me as we drove. The system has failed us. But our bodies got us here the first time. We can survive, you know we can survive, we are living proof.

Marisol was a country girl too. On her own journey she had acted as the mother, even though she was one of the youngest, had been struck by puberty almost before she had time to get used to the idea of it. Where I had let the girls go off alone she had tried to keep everyone together, and like that they had moved through the countryside. I felt ashamed of how I had not cared about what would happen to the other girls. I had just let them go. I had let them walk into whatever disaster was waiting. But then they had done the same to me, too.

My theory, she said, is that they're watching every move we make, and they want to see how well we're doing. Don't lose sight of that. We have a lot to prove.

We drove all through the night, the mountains giving way to twisting woodland. It was very warm. Marisol had heaped bottles of water everywhere in the car; they rolled under the seats, moved from side to side. She held an open one between her thighs, and when it was my turn to drive she periodically reached over and tipped it up to my mouth. I was very aware of her hands near my lips.

From time to time we stopped to pee together, opening the car doors to create a screen. We were bashful about it at first but soon stopped. Our bodies felt both functional and transgressive. There is a person inside of you, I said to Marisol, and she replied solemnly, And inside of you.

Russian dolls, she said, when we had finished laughing. We go on and on and on. Do you ever think what the baby will be like?

I have no frame of reference, I said.

They are two strangers coming to meet us, she said. Are you ever afraid about that?

I am now, I said.

I pictured them not as babies but as two tall, mysterious figures walking towards us from a moon-like landscape.

When we parked, Marisol showed me what was in the boot. Tinned food, packets of pasta and oats, powdered milk and soup, a gas stove and spare canisters, a mess kit. I held up one mysterious package, unmarked. Hot chocolate, she said. Army-issue. High-calorie. I didn't ask where she had got it.

We slept in the car, parked far off the road. Marisol tilted the driver's seat partly back. I prefer to sleep sitting up, like this, she said. Then if they come you're not meeting them at a disadvantage.

Have you seen them? I asked, making a nest in the back out of my sleeping bag.

Sometimes I think I have, she said.

Are you afraid? I asked her.

Only sometimes, she said.

Her breathing slowed. I could not sleep with her right there. I ran through our interactions, the times she had touched me or looked at me, an inventory, trying to solve her. Nothing could be taken for granted. Her hair tipped over the headrest, skull at an angle. I felt protective towards her neck. I reached out to touch the very ends of her hair and fell asleep, eventually, curled up like that in the cold blue.

16

We stopped in a roadside bar the next night to use a real toilet and eat some food. Marisol ordered glasses of weak beer. It's fine, she said, when she caught me looking anxious. It's a decoy. She lifted up her glass and drained half of it in one go, smooth, her throat bobbing.

I sipped at my own and surveyed the room from our table in the corner. It was busy at that time of the night. The men were older than us, leaning into their drinks, into pools of orange lamplight. No bright lights here, that was why Marisol had picked it. One woman sat at the end of the bar, body disguised in a shapeless dark dress that reached to her ankles, light hair in a braid, and I thought she could be one of us, suggested it to Marisol, who turned to her, frowned, shrugged. Our food came, cooked meats and hard bread, pickles. Thank you, Marisol said. Her smile was a beam, cold and true. She would need to watch that, I thought. The barman was stunned by it. Let me know anything else you need, girls, he said. Anything at all. He went back to the bar but I could tell he was watching us. Under the table, I scored the wood once then twice with the knife from my pocket, before putting it back. I'm going to the bathroom, I told Marisol.

I opened the door to the bathroom and was suddenly on the ground. Arms wrapped around me, a hand against my mouth. I tried to bite but my teeth could not gain purchase. Sour skin, my reflexes not up to scratch.

I know what you are, said a woman's voice. Her hand moved to my throat and squeezed, fingers in the soft spaces under my jawbone. I bucked my body, tried to fold in half like a horse throwing its rider. My elbow made contact with her stomach and she grunted, her grip loosening slightly. I did it again, driving my body into hers, and as she rolled away, I hooked my arm with new strength around her neck. I pulled us both up and scrabbled for the knife in my pocket, pressing it roughly to her throat. It was the blonde woman from the bar. Greenish light from one bulb, all that blackness outside compressed into one thin window near the ceiling, no way to get outside from here. I was shaking. Our eyes met in the mirror. Her face contorted, and she hissed at me.

The door swung and someone came in. It was Marisol. Help me, I said, you have to help me. Marisol froze. The woman struggled in my arms and opened her mouth, but I pressed the knife closer. Make a sound and I won't hesitate, I whispered. I watched in the mirror the blade indenting soft skin. If I did cut her throat there would be no denying it, I would watch myself do it, and I wondered if I had it in me, to gut or be gutted with the act reflected back at me, the fear in the woman's eyes, the blood pouring over my hands, and I thought *Yes, yes I do, maybe I didn't always, but I do now.*

Help me! I implored Marisol again. Why are you just standing there?

She blinked, then snapped into action, undoing her belt. Hands behind your back, she told the woman. She wrapped it around and around her wrists, tying it as tightly as possible. We pushed the woman to the ground together and I held her there with the weight of my pregnant body. The woman looked right at me. She was whispering words

I couldn't hear and didn't want to hear, as if praying or cursing. Shut up, Marisol said without looking up from her handiwork. When she was done, the woman immediately started to writhe in an attempt to escape, but only succeeded in flopping on to her stomach. Marisol pulled a wedge of paper towels from the dispenser and pushed them into the woman's mouth as a gag. Her teeth bit down, saliva wetted them into solid mulch. We dragged her with some difficulty into a cubicle. Her legs poked out from the bottom, but there was nothing to be done about it.

Marisol kicked her. That's what you get for being a fucking bitch, she said, amiably, as if discussing the weather. She kicked her again, harder.

Enough, I said.

The woman's eyes were wide and livid. We washed our hands and walked out of the bathroom and picked up our bags. Marisol paid the bill, cool as anything, while I started the car, gripped the steering wheel until my fingers were numb.

17

We drove on and on, sleeping in snatches. The discomfort of the car might have been a problem if we were not so weary, our bodies working overtime. Through the night we had to roll down the windows to keep the cold air at our faces like water, playing the radio, playing the old tapes we had discovered in a box under the passenger seat. Strings and strange beats. Music from a long time ago. We alternated driving and napping, one face intent on the road while the other went soft and slack, headlights dividing the countryside into slices. Every time there was a car behind us we craned our necks to look. We swept back on ourselves, took deserted roads and tortuous routes. It was exhausting.

One afternoon, Marisol pulled over and jabbed at her map. We're burning out, she said. We need a place to lie low, to rest and re-evaluate, somewhere safe. Just for a night or two.

You mean like a hotel? I said.

No more hotels, she said. I still can't believe you were using them.

I suppose I just like the luxurious lifestyle, I said, and she laughed, sharply, at me.

At the edge of a vast stretch of woodland we parked the car. Marisol packed her things efficiently; I scooped mine into my pack with no care.

There's been no rain, she said. We can hide our tracks. We know how to do this.

We walked for a long time. The squirrels were loud, their blundering movements making us halt. We didn't speak, just mouthed words and indicated with our hands. Here? Further? Where?

We came to a stream and pitched our tents on the hard earth beside it. I set a fire and boiled water to make tea and packet soup, as Marisol scoped out our surroundings. She was fast and sharp as a bird. I saw the possibilities for a new and generous mode of surviving in the way she put a hand on a trunk as if to ask its permission.

How did you get rid of the wire? I asked her, when the fire was mainly embers. We could only see a little of the sky where we were. The shape of her was dark across from me.

Someone did it for me, she said. The father. We were stupid. I gave up everything. I annihilated my life with how much I loved him, with the idea of our family together. But he couldn't handle the reality, what it is to run and be chased. He didn't like what it brought out in me. And so I'm here.

I wondered what R would think if he could see me now, lean and wild-eyed, the survival mechanisms kicking in. But then he had never known me before the dark feeling. The blue-ticket woman he thought he had been safe with was always something else underneath, instinct twisting below the surface, setting things in motion.

I wondered what the white-ticket women felt. Were they fulfilled and serene in their purpose, or did they, too, see the world as a sharp, cutting thing; did they, too, have a dark feeling under their skin, pulsing with violence? Did our transformations unite us, make us one, fix whatever was missing in me? Or was I always going to be less? How many ways were there to be a mother?

Marisol looked at me, properly looked at me. It seemed that nobody had ever done so before in my life, that any other gaze had merely skimmed over my skin like a breeze. There was nowhere to hide from her but I did not have the urge to run.

You seem sad, she said.

Something like that, I said.

She reached over and put her hands on my face briefly, then picked up my locket where it lay on top of my jumper and opened it without asking me. I inhaled, but didn't stop her. She took out the crumpled white scrap, smoothed it out, put it in the palm of her hand. She frowned briefly, then smiled.

Hey, she said. I understand. But you don't need this. Put the other one back where it belongs.

I retrieved the blue ticket and restored it, carefully, to its rightful place. For the second that the locket was open and empty, I felt loose and dangerous, unmoored with the knowledge that I could be anyone.

Rip it up, she said, giving me the white one. Rip it as small as you can manage. You're not one of them.

We watched as the pieces flew to the ground like snow, like confetti.

In the morning I swilled my mouth with water and the tooth was looser than ever. I walked away from the tents and knelt in the leaves and the soil, and I wrenched the tooth out with my fingers. It hurt less than I expected. My mouth filled with blood that I spat out. I poured water over the tooth in my palm until it and my hand were clean. When I returned I showed it to Marisol like some kind of proof.

It's a talisman, she said, folding my fingers over it. Keep it safe.

So I slipped it in my jacket pocket next to the knife, and the two objects knocked against each other, their own kind of communion. Fragility and a hard edge. What I had lost, and what I had found.

Cabin

I

We found the cabin in the afternoon, not far from the water. Green light, overgrown. At first we thought it was a mirage. We circled the perimeter, cleared long grass and foliage. The door was chained but Marisol used a hairpin to pick the padlock. She showed me how she did it, reminded me, for once upon a time I had known that skill too.

Vines grew through a broken window in a tiny back bedroom, but in the second bedroom the glass had held, and there were damp-smelling single mattresses in both. A main room with a sink and a built-in cupboard, empty except for one abandoned, pink glove. And a bathroom like the one in the house I had grown up in. Silty dirt and mould on the windowsill. Long spiders running their way to the plughole when we entered the room. I let myself stand in the quiet as if in a trance. I was forever being returned against my will. I would be leaving and returning my whole life. A cockroach ran across the floor; I put out my shoe and crushed its body.

That night we watched the sky darkening gradually. We kept it dark inside too, paranoid about attracting attention. No matches. Marisol put her finger to her lips every time I tried to speak. Quiet, quiet, she said. She doled out playing cards from a pack she had found in the glove compartment of the car. I wanted to ask more about her but I lay still on my sleeping bag, pressing my hands over my lips to keep the words in. Guess, Marisol mouthed at me, indicating the cards, before turning them over. I got two correct. Queen of hearts. Three of diamonds. She touched my hair. It grew too dark to see and we climbed inside our sleeping bags. Moon through the window, lowing wind. I stayed awake listening to her breathing for as long as I could.

As I lay there I thought about what the lottery might have seen or not-seen inside me. What had been recorded and observed and commented upon for my whole life; the times I refused to play, or pulled someone's hair, or buried dolls in the dirt. Had someone been watching when I chopped worms in half to see them regenerate; or when I touched myself under the covers of my bed in that cottage where I grew up, shamed and shameful, not even bleeding yet, a cavalcade of strange and intense images like the movement of water; or when I went into the forest and cried and drove my fists into knots of bark, scratched at my skin with brambles, pressed nettles to my shins and ankles? Was it ordained for me even then?

I should have spent my time in quiet contemplation and healthful pursuits. I should have smiled more, batted away the hand of the boy in the cinema, been less of that shadowy small person, watchful, waiting, dirt under her nails. The path of my life had been already unspooling.

In the morning I took my own pulse and found it full as a drum. More blood in my body. My legs went faster. I had a real reason to run. I should have liked to put on the old nylon shorts and do laps around the woods, avoiding holes and roots, testing the new capacity of my lungs in my changing body. I should have liked to live this new life within my old life. To await R coming in the door with yellow flowers, with a basket of apples. Pram ready in the hallway. Our life expanding to fit the new shape.

But there was only this.

2

We had meant to stay a night, maybe two. Suddenly we had been there for a week, and then longer. The lassitude seeped into our bones. It was hard to move on from somewhere like that. From the quiet that lay on the trees after rain fell, the earth muffled with brown leaves and pine needles.

Every day Marisol said it was time to think of leaving, but when it came to actually go she was as unconvinced as me. Let's lie low, she said, eventually. Something is telling me to stay.

Like what? I challenged. What is speaking through you?

But I didn't want to go either. I wanted to stay there for ever, in the same state of almost-motherhood. A state of possibility rather than reality.

I dreamed one night that I vomited up four objects wrapped in pearlescent membranes, each object wriggling. Each membrane contained a small spiked creature that pushed itself through into the world. They were dark purple, beetle-like. As I watched them they ran away into the grass and the earth. It took a while for me to realize it was a dream, and not something that had happened. I could feel them in my throat, almost taste them. It would not even have surprised me. There was nothing my body could do that would surprise me, now.

One represents you, Marisol said, when I told her about it. One represents me. The other two represent our babies.

She turned away from me to do something. To pour water into the one clouded glass we had found under the sink. I felt struck down by every movement she made. It was not unpleasant.

Maybe, I said.

I considered falling to the ground and kissing her feet, toe by toe. She was flushed, serene. As if this were a place she knew. Her throat rippled as she drank.

Let's measure ourselves, she said when she put the glass down. Let's keep a record to see how much the babies are growing.

We had nothing to measure with, no tape or ruler, so we used our fingers, from knuckle to tip, a private maternal unit of measurement. We counted the circumference of our bumps. Thirty-seven fingers, I said.

Thirty-nine, Marisol said, I'm bigger than you. I'll grow and be as big as the world. She stuck out her arms and I thought about our bodies in communion. I thought about them sending out the echoing signals of whales or bats.

Another day, lying sprawled in the long grass where the cabin's overgrown garden met the forest. We can breathe here, Marisol said. That's something. When was the last time we really breathed? When was the last time we took account?

So we took account. We went deeper into the forest, talked as we moved, so the words felt easier to say.

My name is Calla, and I am going to have a baby. Soon. My name is Calla and this baby is mine.

My name is Marisol and I want to bring something into the world, she said. Something real.

My name is Calla and I want to be a mother because. Because.

I looked up into the sky, up at the leaves, searching for the best reason. It was difficult to think about why I had done it. I had to run at the wall of it, even if it risked breaking me apart.

Because it seemed like everything was telling me it was the right thing to do. Every cell in my body, I said. I tried.

Good, said Marisol. Having a child is both the most rational and irrational decision possible, in this world. This fucking awful, beautiful world, which I can't stop loving, though I have considered it, I have evaluated and counted the ways.

She stopped and kicked a tree stump.

I just wish I had known more, I said to her.

Would it have changed your mind?

I thought about the dark feeling. No, I don't think so, I said.

My name is Marisol and I knew that I would be a good mother. I knew it. I thought I deserved the chance.

My name is Calla and I wanted to choose.

How absurd it had felt to think of myself as a mother even a few years ago. With my wrists as weak as a trussed chicken, and my hollow heart. I had been tired all the time. I did not change my bed sheets. I ate like someone was watching me. Furtive, standing over the sink.

Thinking of yourself like that can be a self-fulfilling prophecy, Marisol said to me when I explained. It doesn't mean you don't deserve it.

She moved slowly, languorously, through a patch of sunlight. We went back to the cabin and in the bathroom we stripped naked and inspected our bodies for ticks. I found one behind her knee and levered it out with tweezers, then crushed it with my thumbnail, left a smudge of blood on her skin. I wanted to press my hot cheek to the back of her thigh and close my eyes, let myself rest there for a second, and so I did.

Oh, the things our bodies could still want us to do, the hope that remained in desire. I knew there was grief stored up in me like water trapped under the ground. I knew that I was never going to be the same, whatever happened. But I was still alive. I was still coursing with blood. I was skinless against the world, its terror, but its beauty too. *Let it into you*, I thought there, in the moments before she pulled me up and kissed me on the mouth for the first time. Let it into you.

3

Another woman came not too long after that, arriving almost as if we had called her. Her name was Lila and the look in her eyes was distant. We heard a crashing in the bushes and ran towards the noise with our pistols out. She fell to her knees. Show us your ticket! we shouted at her, waving the guns at her head.

She opened her locket and we saw blue. She lifted her sweater and we saw flesh curving there. She put her face to the ground and wept hot tears on to earth.

We can't lift you, we explained. You have to walk with us.

We took a hand each and helped her stagger back to the cabin. Pretty name, we told her once she was lying safely inside. She bolted down the hot chocolate we made for her. We stroked her thin hair. It's all right, it's all right, we told her. We helped her to get into the yellow bathtub and soaped her matter-of-factly with water heated on the camping stove, Marisol taking the front and I the back. She shivered in the air, angled her arms around herself. Lift up to the ceiling, we said. Stretch. We rinsed her armpits, the back of her neck, as gently as we could.

Lila was less far along than us. Thirty-five fingers. She had been trying to keep track, but she was not sure of the accuracy. We showed her how to measure and write her findings down in the notebook. Our hands are all different sizes though, she said. The three of us pressed our palms together to compare. There's not much in it, said Marisol, whose hands were smallest.

In the notebook I was writing down lists of names that I no longer had to throw away. I wrote down every name I knew, every likely word that came into my head. I made up words just to fill the space. I wanted to scrawl these names along the walls.

Opal, Cloud, Cedar, Sparrow, Rain, Echo.

You almost had a different name, my father said once. It didn't fit, he said, but he would not tell me what it was, or how he could tell when I was so new and unformed, how a baby was capable of shrugging off a name. This worried me. How a baby was its own person, its own mystery, something I had to protect with everything I had.

4

Lila was the best at the card game. When Marisol laid out the deck
on the floor, she was able to guess correctly almost half the time.
Sometimes she would get five or six in a row. I was jealous of her
intuition and of the attention Marisol gave her because of it, but she
brushed it off. Just guessing, she said, disappearing into the bedroom
where she now slept.

Every day, certain animals came into the garden. We had no real food
for them, only the remnants of whatever had stuck to the pan, which
we shook into the grass. Some of the animals I recognized and some
were new. Some were familiar but the wrong colour, white or golden
where I would have expected them to be grey. They were small and
rodent-like. No rabbits.

The animal chorus, Marisol called them. She liked to go and watch
their approach. We did not think of catching them or eating them. Their
noses twitched. Animals have souls too, you know, said Marisol. I was
not even sure if I believed in souls; or, if they did exist, whether I had
one myself, whether the baby had one. I sat on the ground and watched
her watching them, and when she turned and caught me I flushed. She
went back to the car every few days to check, to move, to bring back
more food. Every time I could make myself quietly frantic at the idea
that she might not return, but she always did, within hours.

She had not kissed me again and we had not spoken about it. But once, when we were sorting dandelion leaves together, she put her hands on my hands. Like this, she said, demonstrating, sousing the leaves in the container with water, massaging them gently to lift off the dirt. She put her head on my shoulder for a second, and I felt myself beautiful suddenly, like a flare of light.

When I combed my hair in the mornings I noted that it was growing back faster than expected. With my small knife I cleaned, very carefully, under my nails. I knew it was animal behaviour to groom yourself as a self-soothing activity, a neutral space between fight and flight.

The dark feeling was still there inside me. It was quieter, but I knew that, underneath, the pulse of it was growing as my pregnancy progressed. I understood it now not as an enemy, but a kind of symbiosis. Sometimes I visualized the dark feeling as an animal inside myself. It would be like smoke made real, but with fur, teeth. It did not seem merely theoretical given, of course, that there was literally another animal inside me already. I imagined the two of them nestled up together in the warm red cave of my body, in love with each other and familiar.

5

The three of us stayed quiet and devotional in the days, standing guard. But when the baby moved for the first time, I could not stay silent.

Look! I shouted to the two women. Look!

There was nothing to see, really, but I pulled my jumper and my T-shirt over my head and walked into the garden in my bra, my skin goose-pimpling with the strangeness of it. Bubbling, twitching movement, but no dents or shapes pushing my skin out.

I swear it was happening, I told them both when they arrived. Marisol put her hands on my stomach. Lila hung back. Her hair was wet. She had been bathing in the stream, had run up the whole way when she heard me call. You can touch, I told her, but she was shy and maybe afraid.

Mine hasn't moved yet, she said.

Mine neither, Marisol said. Soon they will.

It felt strange to be the first, for once. For the rest of the morning I tried to provoke a response from the baby. I jumped lightly on the spot and stretched out my body on the floor, stood with my ankles in the cold stream, hoping the temperature would trigger something in me.

In the afternoon I walked alone through the trees, distracted, longing to feel the movement again. The proof, the otherworldliness. I stuck my face up into the light. I remembered what it had been like to be in the forest before. To lie down on the floor, on earth and foliage. To sleep a long time under the leaves.

That night, Marisol finally came to me and pressed her body against mine. I put my hand inside her; I pressed my own face into the mattress and let my shoulders uncurl, my arms reach out over my head. She tasted of citrus, of sour beer. She hissed thinly through her teeth as if I'd bitten her, and so I did. Being touched was painful and raw in its unfamiliarity. I cried afterwards, and she stroked my hair and said, It's all right.

Were you thinking of me when I was thinking of you, on the road? I asked her when I had stopped crying.

Yes, she said. I was.

Words meant nothing, I still knew that, but they gave me comfort anyway.

In the morning, Lila eyed us slyly, like we were her parents. Marisol and I did not speak of it. There was no need. It was just there. It was part of everything falling into place.

Or, to look at it another way: it seemed too good to even look at directly, so I didn't let myself look at it. I let it sit there. I let it just exist.

6

I washed daily in the bathtub: damp rag, body slippery with Marisol's hard yellow soap, a slip of boiled water, shallower than an inch. Marisol came in to sit with me. She liked to see my body in the underwater light of the bathroom, greenish from the foliage growing up outside. I never told her to leave me alone, not once.

Swamp monster, Marisol said, massaging soap into my hair. Queen ant.

I curled my hands into mandibles, then tentacles. I splashed the water on to her until she was soaked, but she remained uncomplaining. She stretched up and took off her light cotton sundress, pale pink, darker where the water had hit it. Underneath she wasn't wearing anything. The hair running down from her navel and covering her legs was a comforting fur. She got into the bathtub with me with some difficulty. Our stomachs were looking fantastical already, and with her long hair tied on top of her head her proportions seemed even stranger. I didn't know how much tighter my skin would have to stretch. I didn't know when the baby would come. I didn't know a thing. Sometimes this could feel liberating.

Did you love the father? Marisol asked.

Not sure, I said truthfully. Did you?

Yes, she said. She scooted the water around with her hands, put them on my shins. Are you jealous?

No, I said, and again it was the truth. She moved her hands down to my ankles and left them there, holding them as if they were wrists, as if she were about to lead me somewhere.

Do you think the father thinks about you and the baby? she asked, leaning towards me.

No, I said.

I wished I'd had some sort of signal when it happened all those months ago. Some sort of acknowledgement of conception's strange magic. The spark of a fire against dry leaves. The things that happened to your body without you realizing.

Maybe I did love him a little, I said. But he couldn't do it.

She kissed my wet hair. She kissed my mouth with her own mouth open.

He can go fuck himself, she said when she pulled away from me. They can all go fuck themselves.

7

Marisol had a craving for strawberries, so I took Lila out to find some, as a surprise. During our foraging we heard a rustling, a sniffling. We thought it could have been an animal and we almost ran, but then there was a moan that sounded too human. We pushed through into a clearing and found a woman, lying on the ground. She seemed hurt at first, but she was just lost, dehydrated, overcome with it all. She cried a lot at us, in fear and then relief. We gave her water and helped her back with us, with some hesitation. I'm Therese, she said unprompted. I'm pregnant.

Well, don't go telling everyone, Lila said, as we pulled our new arrival through the undergrowth.

Marisol didn't say anything about risk or about resources, though another mouth would be an imposition. Instead she inspected Therese's locket. Once more we boiled water as a woman sat, stripped and cold, in the bathtub. Once more we washed her together, briskly. The glass fogged up. She was tense at first but soon relaxed. Thank you, she said, as I rinsed her hair with water. I've come such a long way, you really wouldn't believe the journey I've had. But I clearly didn't want to know about her journey, and she fell quiet, let us finish our work.

Afterwards, the four of us sat in the dark space of the main room. Our old lives seemed a long way away. The city felt like something from a film, somewhere I had never really been. I thought maybe I had never left the wild country after all, that my life in the city had been a delusion triggered by a parasite, that all along underneath I had been here.

In the cold morning dew, Marisol and I went out alone, before the others were awake. We sat on the grass and kissed. Birds were singing, liquid and unafraid. Marisol aimed her pistol at them but did not shoot.

When will we go to the border? I asked.

Soon, she replied. But not today.

Maybe I will go alone, I said, unconvincing even to myself.

Oh no, she said. Come on. Don't leave me with them. She pulled me down on to the grass so that my head rested on her bump. I could hear her heart, or the baby's heart, or both in tandem.

If these women can find us, the emissaries can too, I said, the sounds of her body filling my ear, lulling me almost against my will.

Trust me, she said, again.

When we got back, Therese accosted us, asking for some hair. Just a few strands, she said. Her eyes were very bright, the blue of a young child, filled with water. When we asked she said it was to perform a ritual. We came outside to watch her do it, cradling our bumps. She walked around the cabin three times with her eyes closed, slowly, feeling her way. She lit a match and held it to the hair, dropping it; the hair went up in smoke instantly and dissipated. She opened her eyes to ours. Done, she said. It smelled evil.

Where did you learn that? we asked her.

I made it up, she said.

I hope you didn't curse us, Lila said. She sat in the corner, her wiry legs crossed as if meditating, whittling little shapes out of wood. I checked what they were later, when they were scattered across the floor – fish, different kinds. The soles of her feet were filthy.

Well of course not, Therese said, though she seemed nervous.

We can each make our own magic, Marisol said.

That evening the women squabbled over food. Therese had taken more without asking: rice and tinned tomatoes, all our portions exactly the same size for fairness's sake, though we were living proof of how fairness could fail a person. Lila had snatched the pot back from Therese and thrown it to the floor, and Therese had cried.

Where are the fathers of your babies? Therese asked, when things were calmer.

Mine left, Marisol said shortly.

Mine never came at all, I said. He won't even speak to me on the phone.

I don't know mine, Lila said, shrugging. I never tended to have long-term things. If you know what I mean. I'm not actually totally sure who he is.

No judgement, obviously, said Marisol.

Mine will come for me, past the border, Therese said. We are going to have a new life together. He said I should go and I should be brave, he'll find me there.

She seemed peaceful. Marisol leaned into me, almost imperceptibly. I saw Lila's eyebrows move up towards her hairline, but nobody said anything.

Therese had brought along a nail file made of frosted glass and a pink bottle of varnish. She did the nails on our hands for us but did not do our toes. I hate feet, she said. They make me nauseated.

I thought about the man in the last hotel and agreed. Blew on my own fingers and then on Marisol's too, to make them dry faster.

Doesn't it remind you of the first days in the city? Marisol asked me that night, as we lay next to each other. The window was wide open and it was so dark that it felt like being underwater, no stars in the sky. All us women together in one place.

I'd rather leave that behind, I said.

That first winter in the city – it had been like a meal laid out for you. What do you want to do with your life? they asked. I had taken the required tests in a large cream-painted hall with plate-glass windows hot from the sun, several others around the same age sitting ahead and behind me in rows. By arriving alive, we had proved something about ourselves already. The teachers giving out the papers were tender towards us, letting their hands linger on the wooden desks with names carved in. There were maths and science questions but philosophy too, and theorems harder than any I had encountered at school. I did my best and eventually I received a piece of paper setting out my options. It was a kind of resuming. The lottery and the journey and the recovering were just dead space, a stutter, a bad dream. Just something you had to get through and then your life, the one you deserved, was yours again.

I was sleeping back then in a building full of other blue-ticket girls also recovering from the journey. The bedroom walls were yellow for good health and mind. Every afternoon we were allowed to lie there in repose. I pinned up pictures of flowers that I cut from a magazine with safety scissors, taking great care around the edges, and we had mosquito nets above the beds. There was a hard and piercing happiness in that room. The happiness of having made it, with the rest of life there to step into.

We were not in that room any more. Marisol wrapped herself around me. She put her hand to my throat. I didn't know how she knew I would like that. Afterwards, when she kissed my forehead, I was wet and ashamed.

8

Now the baby moves you must give it a name, the others said when I woke up the following day. They had already breakfasted and seemed to have been discussing me. You can't just keep calling it Baby.

We can help you choose, Therese offered, hopeful. She followed Marisol and me around like a dog. It was hard to like her, though I knew this was ugly of me.

I spent some time in silence that afternoon with my list, in the garden, batting flies away from my face. It felt like a decision too big for anyone to make but there I was, making it.

I chose, but I don't want to tell anybody the name, I said when I came back in, the door swinging behind me. Not until the baby is born. Everyone shrugged, but left me alone. It felt good to have that kind of secret inside of me – nothing sordid, nothing damaging. A little sun-warmed stone in my stomach.

I'm your mother, I said to the baby later in private, but coming out of my mouth it seemed presumptuous. Someone was going to call me out on it. Mother, I tried out again, flushing bright red.

When we remembered, we measured our bellies again and wrote the figures down. We put up a tent in the main room so that there was somewhere to be alone, a pocket of privacy in the claustrophobia of the cabin. At night I slept on the bare mattress breathing in the smell of Marisol's hair, the shape of her skull tucked under my chin.

9

We need more supplies, Marisol said one day. We'll have to find a supermarket. It might take some time.

I don't want you to go, I said, privately. It's not safe. Send one of the others.

I had started to indulge the dream of staying in the woods for ever. Of raising my child on trapped rabbits, berries, the occasional chocolate bar. I wondered who the baby would look like, and whether Marisol and I would raise our children as siblings, build the cabin into something beautiful, bend the landscape to our needs. I was embarrassed by my own sentimentality. As if she would want to do that with me.

We're all hungry, Marisol said. We need to look after our health. And there are only a few tins left in the car. She touched her hand to my cheek. Don't worry, she said, kissing me on the corner of the mouth.

We drew blades of grass to decide who would stay; me and Therese picked the two longest pieces. We waved the others off at the door.

Marisol and Lila were gone all day. Therese sat on the floor, eyes closed, as if meditating. Night fell without them and brought a hard rainstorm which revealed leaks in the roof. We found what we could to collect the water, empty cans and containers, but it was not much good. Therese was slow, and I lost my patience and shouted at her. I didn't always like that hardness in me. I didn't think I had always been cruel. I apologized to Therese but she sulked, crawling into the tent, the safe zone, and when she came out it looked as if she had been crying. The rain would not have dared to come in if Marisol were there, I believed. She would repel it, cause the clouds to seal up. Through the night I thought intently of her beautiful face. I felt feverish, overwrought. In the morning there was still damp everywhere; ants swarmed the ground and we had to beat them away with our shoes. The animal chorus gathered on the lawn but Marisol was not there to watch or to feed them, so they dispersed.

That afternoon, when the ants had gone and the sky was grey but holding, I sat on the bubbled orange linoleum of the bathroom floor with my white underwear in my hands. There was pinkness spotting the fabric, the way there had been that day back in the city. I drew my knees up as far as I could to my body. The baby wasn't moving.

All this to end here, I told Therese very quietly when she came to find me after an hour, knocking on the door until I opened it. All the things left behind only to end like this.

Therese knelt down on the floor with me. Come on. It could be normal, she said, reaching out her arms, and I surprised myself by letting her hold me. It could really be nothing, she repeated. Who knows what our bodies are supposed to be doing right now.

It's because I'm not fit to be a mother, I told her. I knew my body would win over in the end.

That's not true, Therese said. That's absolutely not true.

It was the first time I had said it out loud to someone. Of course Therese would say it wasn't true, because she was in the same boat. If we didn't have belief, we had nothing. I hated her a little, again, even with her kindness.

Tell me about your happiest day, Therese said. She held my hands in hers, tightly.

I told her about the day I got my first job. How I received the call and then I walked through the city in the way that was becoming a part of my routine, and it was one of the summer days where the air is clear, where there's the promise of a long evening and joy inside it. I met a friend at a bar and we sat outside. We talked for a long time and ate small bitter olives. Everything filled me. It wasn't a remarkable day. But the warmth; the possibility. Later I walked home by the canal. There was a beauty in my solitude. I thought I might never be lonely again.

That's a good one, Therese said. A good one.

There was nothing to be done. I put on clean underwear and took the bloodied ones to soak in the stream. With the pistol cold in my hand I walked to a distance away in the trees and pressed it to my head. It was real and it was solid. I considered my options. I considered the idea that I had brought it on myself. I let the gun fall back to my side. When I felt the baby move, I had to sit down with the shock.

Don't do that to me, I said to the baby, privately. I was talking to them always by then, the way I had talked to myself before. Maybe I had always been talking to them.

You can't do that to me, I said to them. You can't.

I O

Marisol and Lila arrived with food in their packs and another woman, but it was different this time. Blood was jammy at her temples, her eye was swollen purple, though she seemed hostile rather than afraid. I was so fixated on her injuries that it took me a while to notice that she did not seem to be pregnant. They led her into the bathroom. She protested at first as we stripped her clothes and shoes off, businesslike. She slapped my hands away as I undid buttons. I glimpsed the sharp plane of her hipbones. Fine, do it yourself, I said.

She's a white-ticket, Marisol explained. We found her near the road.

Marisol stayed to watch over her in the bathroom. In the other room the rest of us unpacked bags of rice and pasta, oranges and lemons to guard against scurvy, tinned tomatoes, large bars of dark chocolate, and asked Lila what had happened.

We were driving, obviously, took a long route but found a supermarket in the end, she said. We got what we needed. And then on the way back we saw something by the road, like a pile of rags, and it was moving. I wanted to drive past but Marisol stopped the car to investigate. We couldn't leave her there.

I knocked at the bathroom door with clean clothes, and Marisol opened it a crack. Is everything okay? I asked her, passing her the things. Yes, she said. Her eyes were soft and wet. I couldn't hear movement from the bathtub. Marisol turned away, closed the door.

The white-ticket woman was called Valerie. That evening she had recovered enough to come and sit with us. We sat formally, straight-backed. We were wary. She took off her locket as a peace offering and put it on the floor in front of her.

Pass it around if you like, she said. So we did, we passed it from person to person, we opened up the clasp and saw the clean whiteness inside. It did not burn us when we touched it. It did not leave a mark.

Put it on, if you like, she repeated, and so we took off our lockets one by one and tried on hers. It felt heavier around my neck.

Are you pregnant? Lila asked.

I was, she said. But I'm not any more.

Did you want to be pregnant? Therese asked, leaning forward.

No, said Valerie. Not at all.

She told us how when she realized what was happening she went to her doctor, who showed her the baby moving on a screen in the clinic. She was shown the heartbeat. Unlike the conversations we had known, Valerie's doctor would not do anything about it. But we knew more than anyone how there were ways to go against the body, to make offerings of blood.

How did you do it? asked Lila. She looked ghoulish, more animated than I had ever seen her before.

I don't want to talk about that, Valerie said.

We sat there and listened and we were very still.

My husband found out. He didn't believe that it was an accident. He was disgusted with me. But it wasn't his body.

She spoke as if reading from a list she had gone over many times, as if she were used to parading her reasons, if only to herself. She smiled briefly, but it didn't reach her eyes.

He'll take me back. What else can he do?

My right hand held on to my left hand very tightly. Bone on bone.

What was it like for you to be pregnant? asked Therese.

It was like nothing, she said. It was just another state of the body. I was sick for a month. And then it was over, like it had never happened.

But something did happen, said Lila.

But it was like nothing had happened, Valerie said. Or it could have been. Being found out was my only mistake.

Her knuckles were white.

I stand by that statement, she said, though none of us had questioned it.

Be kind to Valerie, Marisol told me afterwards, in bed.

Valerie was asleep in the tent. She was the lowest priority physically. That was just how biology dictated it.

She's like us but different, she said. She did what she had to do.

I had seen the spark of it, the kinship. There was an animal somewhere in Valerie too, a dark feeling. It had opened something up to her, made her decision possible. But I still didn't trust her.

You can trust her, Marisol said, as I knew she would. I have an instinct for people.

Instinct isn't always right, I countered. Marisol leaned on her elbow and looked at me in a shaft of moonlight.

Then what are we doing here? she said.

In a way we're going against our most basic instinct, I said. The one for self-preservation.

I don't look at it that way, she said.

The cool darkness around us, the sounds of breathing from the other rooms.

I told Marisol about the bleeding that had passed over me as suddenly as the thunderstorm, how the fear had gutted me, how it had reminded me of all there was left to lose. I told her about the dark feeling. Did you feel it too, in your own way? I asked, eager, too eager.

She took my hand. Yes, she said, I felt it too. I felt it every second of every day. I feel it now. Like a beating heart inside my own heart, stronger all the time.

We couldn't sleep. We went outside to see the moon, sat in the grass. She leaned back, tucked her feet under herself.

You've never told me about your old life, I said. She paused for a second, then another.

You've never told me about yours, she said.

Well there's nothing really to tell, I said. You never asked.

I suppose I think it's not important, she said. None of that really matters now.

But I still told her about sterilizing petri dishes, about going to the bars and swimming in the cold turquoise water with the cap pulled down low over my ears. I told her about walking around the city in the very late night or very early morning, how it was my favourite time, when dawn started stippling the sky and that city we had lived in seemed pure and empty, something waiting to be stepped into.

That life feels so small, she said. So far away.

Tell me something, I said. Just one thing.

She stared at her hands. There is something I should tell you, but I don't want to do it. You might leave if you know.

I won't, I promised, rashly.

Maybe you should, she said. She paused, closed her eyes.

I was a doctor, she said. Don't say anything for a second.

I tried to picture her in the doctor's coat, and it was easy. Her hair tied back neatly and dark cotton clothes underneath. She would pull the latex gloves on to her hands and calm people down with soft words, her hands at their temples, teasing out their secrets, their thoughts. I was stupid not to have seen it. Her eyes opened and found mine, inscrutable. She placed her fingers on my arm.

Don't touch me, please, I said. Her hand lifted right away.

See, now you want to go, she said. She seemed calm, regardless.

I did want to go, I wanted to run into the trees and never come back.

That was my old life, she said. You've left things behind too.

I stood up, told her I was tired and going to bed and that she could follow me there, but that first I needed some time to think. Sit here and wait, I said. She remained, looking up at the sky.

Later on, when I was almost asleep, I heard her come to the bed. I heard her whisper, Nobody is immune, that's what you have to understand, I didn't want to be like this, I didn't ask for any of this.

What does it feel like? I asked. What did it feel like?

Heavy, she said. Like a weight you carry around always.

11

It was strange to be around Valerie. We couldn't help but resent her. Over breakfast we stared at her until she refused to meet our eyes any more. Her appearance had brought with it reminders of what we had shucked off; our voices subdued as we grappled with what she represented, as we worried about her judging our personalities and behaviour.

Childbirth is a kind of death, she said as we watched her. Can you blame me for not wanting to take that on?

None of us answered. Even Therese was quiet. We ate granola mixed with water and powdered milk. We tried to explain to Valerie that we were intrinsically wary because she had been found worthy all those years ago where we were somehow lacking.

I don't see it like that, she said. If anything, I'm the one found lacking. All my life I've been told I can only be complete if I grow something inside of me and bring it into the world. Whereas you are whole and perfect as you are.

Her breath came in short bursts.

I never thought of it like that, said Marisol, mildly. Thanks for your perspective.

After breakfast, Marisol broke the news about what she was.

Go, if you want, she said. I'd understand.

Lila and Therese swapped glances, but what could they do? Where else to go?

Our old life is gone. Let's not dwell on who we used to be, said Marisol.

We watched, through the window, Valerie sitting outside on a patch of grass. Smoking one cigarette and then lighting a second before the first was even done, stubbing it out on the ground. Lila was standing next to me. She licked her lips.

There was a lot of instant gratification in that life that we can no longer experience, Marisol explained.

You mean it's hard to be good all the time, Lila said. She smiled suddenly. I used to be very raucous, she said. Me too, I agreed. Me too, Therese piped up, not wanting to be left out. I tried to picture them shrieking at the night sky, drinking shots of clear alcohol, dancing until they fell to the floor. It was difficult. Their faces were drawn, hair pulled tight. Everybody looked tired, no matter how long they slept. There was no mirror, but I imagined it was the same for me.

In my head I imagined things Doctor A might say. *Who would want to bring a child into this world? What does it say about you?*

I suppose I wanted to leave something on this earth, I said to the ghost of him.

Try harder, the ghost said back.

It was strange to have thoughts of him resurfacing. Perhaps intimacy under duress counted for something after all, had bonded us in a way I could never escape. Though if I were truthful with myself I could hardly picture his face. There was a strange grief to realizing that, like walking past someone you used to love, in the street.

In the night I sat up and thought there was a dark shape coming for us, but it was just a sheet I had hung up to dry. It was just nothing at all.

12

It was my turn to go for supplies. The other women did not want me to go because I was showing the most, but we didn't have enough food to gain the weight we were supposed to, and besides, I was desperate to get out. The leaves were pressing down on me. Lila came with me, because she knew where the car was. I wore the maternity dress from the town with the lake, a little too big for me still, hanging loose over my new body. My hair was just about long enough for Valerie to do it in the white-ticket fashion – tied back neatly at the nape of the neck. Her hands were smooth. In my head I recited a telephone number. I ran the numbers up and down like an arpeggio, like fingers down a spine. Marisol watched me as I put the pistol in my jacket pocket. The women waved us off.

Lila was grim and silent in the forest as we walked. Occasionally she put a hand on my arm and motioned – *this way*. The trees gave way to road and field so quickly that it felt like a trick, our shelter as flimsy as a piece of cardboard. In the car itself Lila relaxed. She checked inside the boot and under the seats. I felt very affectionate suddenly, towards her anxious hands, chapped skin, the practised way she observed and took note.

Lila rifled through the glove compartment for anything useful and found a half-full packet of cigarettes. I'd love one of these, she said, wistfully, studying the branding.

Let's share one in the car park, I suggested. Nobody else has to know.

So we did, lighting one up and sitting together in the car, passing it back and forth, watching the men and women go in the automatic doors. The taste was too strong and the rush of it made me break out in a sweat. The baby kicked in protest. Lila opened her car door, dropped the stub to the dirt and ground it decisively under the heel of her boot, and I liked her even more.

In the supermarket we pushed a large silver trolley under bright lights. The squeaking wheel was still audible even with the cheerful blare of the music. It seemed like a cacophony, so used was I to stillness. There were no emissaries on guard this far out. In the cereal aisle I lied to Lila about needing the bathroom. Of course, she said. It was outside of the supermarket, in a brick outhouse. I wavered by the door and then walked toward the orange plastic telephone booth beside it, as I knew I would, and dialled.

I thought you might be dead, Doctor A said when he came on the line. Relief overcame me. It made my legs shake.

How would that make you feel? I asked, winding the cord around my hand, my wrist, cutting off the circulation.

No, I ask how *you* feel, he said.

But you didn't, I replied. I was reminded of the best days of our practice, when I could bounce my antagonism off him, when I could goad and rant, and he would sit there unmoved.

Would that make you sad? I asked. I wanted, so badly, for him to be angry at me, for him to care. I kept watch on the doors in case Lila appeared.

I'm a professional, he said. I would feel impartial about it. I would feel, from a professional viewpoint, that it was a shame, that you're not beyond redemption.

I thought I passed redemption a long time ago, I said. Hearing his voice made me feel giddy.

You might think you're good at survival but you are prone to mistakes, he said.

Is that why I'm a blue-ticket?

You have a one-track mind.

But is it?

I'm just stating the facts, he said. I'm trying to help you by isolating your behaviours. I am reflecting yourself back at you, the way I have always done.

Do you love me? I asked.

Inasmuch as it's my job to love all human creatures, he said. Inasmuch as it's my job to respect and guide them through the darkness of their days.

Bullshit, I said, and I hung up.

I took a second to crouch down and bury my face, very briefly, in my hands. No comfort, less than comfort. It hadn't helped at all and I felt cheated by my impulses, by the queasy anticipation of going over his number the whole journey, reciting it silently as if it had ever held any answers.

But there was no time to waste. I went and found Lila. She was standing, disorientated, at the meat counter, a pack of steak in one hand and sausages in the other. My eyes were drawn to the marbled slabs of red, to the oozing blood. I had to breathe in gulps to keep from retching.

I'm so hungry, Lila said to me. She spoke like a child, all her spikiness dissolved, and I realized with some surprise that she was possibly quite a lot younger than us; I felt the need suddenly to ask her the why and the how and the where, but that was against the unspoken bargain, that our old lives belonged to us and bore no relevance to the present.

I could eat a horse, she said, I could eat a wolf. I could eat anything. I hate this.

I put my hands on her shoulders.

Look at me, I said. Breathe deeply. Let's pay for what we have. Let's go.

The woman scanning our food seemed taken aback at the choices and quantities. I was reminded that every venture into the outside world was a breaching, phone call or no phone call. Lila's eyes were red.

Please pack the heavy things, I asked her, as if everything was normal, as if anything could ever be all right again. What beautiful weather we are having. What a delicious dinner we are going to make when we are home.

13

Tell me about dying and coming back to life, I asked Marisol that night.

In the trees around us I pictured emissaries, closing in. I pictured them shooting orange flares over the forest where we were hiding. We had allowed ourselves to feel safe, but actually there was no safety to be found, and perhaps never had been.

I transferred my sense of loss into touching her, mapping her body, placing my hands on her soft ribcage, shins, stomach. Nervous energy displaced, replaced. You're tiring me, she said.

Tell me, I asked her again.

She was lying down on the bed fully clothed, her arms crossed behind her head. She appraised me. All right, she said finally. If you're sure you want to know.

She told me about the arm laid out for another doctor, the other arm with an IV line into the vein. There was a bag of fluid, a violet liquid injected into her bloodstream.

I was asleep, she said, and then I was awake in a clean white place. It was my childhood bedroom but it was almost completely empty, and everything was full of light. My mother came to me and held my hand. I had not seen her in a long time. I did go and visit her after I had settled in the city, once or twice, but it was never the same as when I was a child. In the dream she loved me again.

In this room there was a grey egg on a white table, she continued. I went to the egg and held it in my hands, and the shell pulsed. It became very important to break the egg. I lifted it up with both hands and I brought it down on to the surface of the table, started to pick away the pieces of the shell. But before I could see what was inside, I was brought back to life.

Very rarely I have dreams that take me back to the room, she said. Often I am on the verge of seeing what is in the egg. I am certain that I will get to see it before I die. And I am afraid to see what is inside it, but also I have been waiting my whole life.

She sat up and reached for her comb. She started to move it with long, deliberate strokes, pulling her hair over one shoulder.

I thought that if I could be a good doctor and person they would change my ticket, she said. I thought that there was a way to prove that you deserved it. That one day they would lead me into another room, a room full of light like the one I had seen, and they would say that I had earned my right to choose. I tried my best to demonstrate my suitability, I tried to be maternal at every opportunity. But there is no choosing.

That's enough, I said to her. I put both my hands on her face.

Do you love me, she asked later, after we had fucked. We were breathing hard as if we had been chasing each other. It sounded like a statement, not a question.

I couldn't answer satisfactorily. I didn't know how to explain that all my love was bound up in my stomach, that it was contaminated with fear.

Do you love me, I echoed instead, copying her tone, but she had already fallen asleep.

In the morning, before everyone else was awake, I heard a wild dog. It was in the garden and it was making an evil-throated sound. Stop it, I whispered through the window. I could see its teeth bared. I watched as it came further into the garden, searching for an entry point, and I knew it was going to come into the cabin, its eyes wide, ready to rip us all to shreds, we were already dead. *Go away, go away.* Nobody was waking up, I was alone. Therese's gun was on the table, just lying there. I took it up, hesitated, then ran outside. We faced each other, two animals. Our eyes locked. It was going to jump and get my throat. My finger pulled the trigger, and it didn't seem possible that it would work, but it did.

The sound deafened me temporarily, louder than I remembered from the days when my father had showed me how to pick off the pinwheeling shape of birds in the sky. The dog dropped. Dark mist over the forest; ragged panting for a few more moments, and then silence. I thought about its tracks leading out from our cabin into the darkness. The other women found me there, frozen.

It was a demon, I explained. It was like my dreams.

It was just a dog, Marisol said, kneeling over the glossy body. It was just a dog, and now it's over.

14

Without unloading my thoughts to Doctor A, my brain started to feel heavy and sodden. I slept often, sometimes needing to nap even before the sun reached the midday point in the sky, dreaming of two mothers with their faces blending into each other, and was woken by the racing of my heart. Sometimes I woke to Marisol taking my pulse, and her cat eyes trained on my face. There was a weight on my chest.

Real love is a degradation, Marisol said to me one morning. You'll do anything for your child, and I mean anything. Worse things than you've ever imagined.

Her speech was slipping towards the syntax of the doctors, the rhythms of their proclamations. I couldn't stop seeing her like that now. When she arched her back, sighed, there was an edge of revulsion that at once tempered my desire and whetted it. I no longer felt truly safe, I no longer felt truly healthy, but I couldn't turn her away or ignore her or leave. When I thought of leaving all I could see was myself crawling through the forest, on my hands and knees, towards disaster.

She put her hands inside my mouth to search for more loose teeth. Let me pull them, she begged, but I didn't let her, I bit her fingers lightly, until she moved them out, ran them over my chin, my neck.

In the mornings she was luminescent, though she never seemed to sleep any more. She spoke nonsense-words to birds outside our window, went out at dawn to catch the animal chorus, her attention to which no longer seemed a sweet affectation.

I could tell that the other women talked about her, and about me. I was angry because we had taken them in, so they could not say anything about us, they could not judge us or whisper. We had drawn them into our shelter, our quiet world, and they should be grateful for it.

Blue mornings. Lila started to sleepwalk, to thrash inside nightmares. We found her standing on the thresholds of rooms, or the windows and doors were open when we woke, letting in wet rushes of air.

Perhaps it was the baby. Hers had started to move now — she ran in one afternoon, her hair and dress damp with sweat, clinging to her like tissue paper. It feels like magic, she said, clutching at her stomach. I feel seasick.

Oldest magic of all time, said Marisol, coming over from the stove to feel the kicking.

Lila named the baby River. We patted her stomach through her grey cotton dress. We were collaborators and competitors. A sudden ache at the thought that her baby might make it and mine might not, tamped down at once before it could surface too clearly.

Tell us the story of what happens when we get to the border, Lila asked Marisol, who had gone back to the stove and was peering into the pan.

You cross it, she said, not looking up.

But how? Lila asked.

You just walk right across it.

It can't be that easy, she protested.

We were all listening by now.

It can be, Marisol said, but still she wouldn't turn to face us. I watched her shoulders rise then fall.

You cross, and then you take the locket off. Nobody sends their children into the country or follows anyone else around. Nobody has to see a doctor all the time. Only if you want to. Only if you're sick.

I had gone on holiday across the sea once, the only time that my doctor had approved my visa. Back then, a baby had been the last thing on my mind. I would not run off into the sunset and become pregnant and never return, the idea had been laughable. I took a train underneath the water. Every so often a guard would come round and check everybody's tickets and papers and permits. Opening my locket for them felt so intimate. I hated being looked up and down. I had already been inspected before my papers were issued, my legs in stirrups, my old doctor calmly pawing at my cervix.

I had slept through the train journey, head leaning on the cloudy glass of the window. Outside, red earth, like we were emerging on to another planet. It was very hot there, hotter than in our own country. I saw tiny reptiles with sharp teeth in the swampland and on the beaches. In the night, moths stuck to every lamp, some of them with bodies as big as my thumb. I drank cheap blue drinks on the beach and cheap clear spirits in my hotel room, pouring them into the glass where my toothbrush was supposed to rest.

207

Nobody wore lockets there. People spoke to me with curiosity, asking if they could look inside the locket, even asked if they could take my ticket out and see what it was made of, but I drew the line there. They wanted to know how I felt about it and I said it was great, I was very happy in fact, that sometimes choice was not beautiful or necessary but bewildering, that I had lived a good life without thinking *what if, what if.* Sometimes when I was especially drunk I took the locket off and let people pass it around. A small girl took a liking to it; her parents used a disposable camera to take a photograph of her wearing it. Somewhere in the world that photo might still exist. The minutes without it around my neck had made me feel free and naked. Everybody had been very kind to me. I could take the baby back there, perhaps.

The idea made me excited. I floated it to the others. We could go anywhere if we wanted to.

Breakfast time, said Marisol, bringing over our sludge. Let's be quiet for now. This is still in the future. Survival is another country too, and we have to make it there first.

15

In the night and early mornings I started to see strange things. Waking dreams, streaks of light. The shadows in the corners of our room moved and re-sculpted themselves. I drew the knife through the darkness as if something could be caught on the blade. Whatever was happening to Lila was happening to me too. It was catching, a low-grade fever. We couldn't tell if it was normal, something to be expected. What other sickness or state could make our taste buds change, push our hearts against our lungs, set our moods to swinging wildly? I found I no longer wanted to know the details of what was happening inside me, even if it were possible. It was too overwhelming to think about bursting out of myself, new-blooded and transformed. When I looked down at my body, I half expected to see feathers, scales.

I didn't know if pregnancy was a kind of wound, what the body considered it: a state of grace, a state of danger, or both. When I touched a finger to my armpit it came away slick with sweat. The heat came off me like I was a star in a dark sky.

Come back to bed, Marisol said. You need to watch these behaviours. Her voice was gentle but she held me in her arms with a vice-like grip so I could not return to whatever I thought was there. I'm worried about you, she said.

I'm not worried about me, I replied, feeling hard and clean and ready.

You're slipping away from us.

No, I said. I'm here more than ever before. I'm just pregnant.

I wasn't afraid to say the words any more, mostly. *Pregnant*, I said to myself like a dare. *Mother. Mother. Mother.*

Pay attention to yourself, Marisol said. That's all I'm saying.

I waited until she turned over and went back to sleep. I lay awake. The knife wasn't in my hand but lay on the floor, where I could reach it easily if I needed to. Fingertips brushing the handle, the blade.

All night I imagined my baby. Round, peach-downy. How even their worst cries would be a chiming of a note that I held inside myself too. And the knife on the floor, to protect them. My hands of comfort capable of tearing enemies apart. There had been a viciousness in the way I had cried over babies before, in the city, the way I had wanted to run away with them in my arms. And now this urge, to keep them safe at any cost: there was nothing gentle about that instinct. Now that I was there, almost there, grasping for it, the idea of softness felt laughable.

16

Marisol started to offer sessions to the other women. You might as well let me help you, she said. To my surprise they all said yes, even Valerie. I refused, of course. What are you thinking, I said, and she said, I'm thinking about the good I can do, while we're here. I'm thinking about what it means for us to be alone and afraid and how if we can just talk, if we can untangle ourselves, it might help.

Marisol in a mint-green room, weighing somebody, adjusting the counterweight and reading the results out loud for the tape. Marisol observing, as if a brain could be placed in the palm of one's hand and read like a book. Marisol making calls, elegantly and with the minimum of fuss, to the necessary authorities. All the while, the blue ticket around her neck; knowing it was not what she wanted, she must have been able to see into herself from the start, unless even doctors had a blind spot there. I wondered how she felt about mind over matter, about how the two could work together. Even she had been undone by loving someone – that had been her downfall, and there was a comfort in that thought, how could there not be?

I thought about it more and more. And earlier things too. A friend of my father's in the doorway of my room, silhouetted, as I pretended to sleep. Those boys on the road. How I had swum in the mulch of dead leaves and dirt. How I had made the things I was afraid of mine.

How if you can do that, not much can hurt you. The intimacy of someone's hands near your face. Blood on my thighs and thinking *what are you*. The things I didn't want to talk to Doctor A about. The things I felt might confirm to him who I was, might give a name and reason to my badness.

The weight of the air pressed down on me, and yet I was floating. I waited for the women to come back to me. Out there, kneeling in the woods, performing their confessions. Waiting to be absolved, the only way possible. I sat amidst the weeds in the garden or lay on the mattress I shared with Marisol, and let myself fall asleep, waking with a start. Whenever I woke I lay there very still for a few minutes, listening out for anything that would indicate the approach of an enemy, but all I could ever hear were leaves blowing, the birds crying above me.

17

I was restless all the time, that low-level fever again. I woke too early one morning and went to walk in the forest, but Valerie was up too, sitting alone outside on the grass. I'll come with you, we shouldn't go alone, she said, before I could make an excuse. Rain pattered on the grass and leaves, dampened our hair, but neither of us complained.

As we walked I wondered about the baby and what they were feeling or seeing, what strange dreams moved through their mind, whether they were like the ones I experienced, attenuated and filtered through my blood. The trees around me kept switching between beauty and malevolence in the grey early-morning light. Valerie hummed a little tune. It was strange to be alone with her. The curve of her neck. Her skin, even beneath the bruises, was very smooth. She didn't seem so dissimilar to me. Perhaps we could swap selves, walk out of the forest with the lives we wanted. The boundaries of our flesh felt permeable. I pushed through the branches. The sun was coming up; I could feel the first small bursts of heat on my face. I realized it was past midsummer, that I was ripening, moving towards completion or rot. The baby was moving. I stopped, patting my stomach, trying to calm them down.

Can I feel it? Valerie asked, pointing at my stomach, and I lifted up my T-shirt for her. She put one hand on my skin. Oh, that's horrible, she said, starting to giggle, which set me off too. Suddenly it seemed like the funniest thing in the world, to have something alive inside me. And awful too. Her face was soft.

I don't understand why you want to have your body hijacked this way. To embark on such danger. You were lucky not to be picked, you know.

I don't feel lucky, I said.

You are, she said. She pulled her hand away from my stomach.

Would you do it again? I asked. My heart thumped, as if I didn't really want to hear the answer, but also I did want to hear her say it, I wanted the unspeakable to be spoken, I wanted it filling up the forest, the space between us.

Yes, she said. I wouldn't hesitate.

You don't have to have one, I said. The white-ticket women existed on another plane even as we walked past each other in the street, even as we locked eyes, hands brushing in shops or bars or cafés.

I do, she said. Everybody expects it. The doctors. Husband. I don't want any of it. I'd rather die. It's the worst thing you can do to yourself.

Something in you, I said to her. My mouth felt dry and unwieldy, I didn't want to look at her any more. There's something in you that's not in me.

I don't see it, she said. She lifted her hand suddenly, pressed her palm to mine with soft force. Do you see it?

No spark passing between us, no atmospheric disturbance. No indication of the lack. She seemed like a witch. She seemed unyielding and ungrateful. To be chosen in that way and not to understand it, not to value it. I turned away from her. I'm going back, I said.

I expected the others would still be asleep, but as we approached the cabin I saw two figures outside. They were looking down at something. Animal, vegetable, mineral. I ran through the options. Enemy felled. Something come for us finally. One or both of them was crying, a thin noise. Valerie and I glanced at each other, hesitated, before drawing closer.

Soft flesh, wet grass. I saw the shape lying on the ground and I fell to my knees. I realized, too slowly, it was Therese.

This is a dream, said Lila's voice at my side. This is one of the dreams I've been having.

This is not a dream, said Marisol, from the other side.

Belly-down to the ground with arms flung out as if swimming, her long hair making her faceless, strewn across the earth. Around us, all the birds were singing like an alarm. They were waking up to the world.

18

The first thing, the worst thing, was having to discuss whether we could save the baby. Having to turn her over and put our hands on her stomach and feel for movement, for something still swimming in her blood. It was hard to tell. Someone had brought a knife from the cabin and I pictured us cutting the baby out, holding it up by its ankles, shaking air into its lungs. Marisol removed our hands from Therese's skin, gently, one by one.

Slowly, we pieced together the evidence. Large, sharp stone smeared with her blood. The hollow in the mud where her feet had slid, earth loosened by the rain. Lila sat on the ground, put her arms around her legs and stared at the body.

What happened? Marisol asked, crouching down next to her.

I woke up here, Lila said. I don't know how I got outside. I must have heard something, and then I woke up to her like this, fallen. Her teeth chattered, eyes spun. They fixed on me and I had to look away.

Oh God, she said, looking back to the body. She put her head into her hands.

Marisol took in the ground beside Lila, where the knife from her survival kit lay abandoned in the mud. An accident, she said firmly. She went over to Lila, put a hand under her chin and raised up her face so she could look into her eyes. It was an accident, she repeated.

Lila nodded as if in a trance. Yes, she said.

We spent the rest of the day digging a grave. We cleaned up the blood on our hands and knees, and covered Therese with her blanket. Therese's feet stuck out from under it, but when we adjusted the material another part of her was revealed instead. In the end we left it, her toes better than seeing her face.

Lila didn't say anything. She scooped up earth as if it were what she was born to do, as if this were just another one of a hundred graves she had dug. We couldn't get it very deep. When it came to carrying the body out, there was no dignified way to do it. Valerie, as the only non-pregnant woman, took the majority of the weight, lifting her under the armpits. Marisol and I took the legs. Lila supported the torso, the bump. When we reached the grave, it was Valerie that got her into it, sweating, pushing and pulling.

Burying her felt strange and shameful. I wanted to let Therese float down the stream. I wanted to set her aflame. Marisol said a few words.

For Therese. Who was our friend. We are sorry about what happened. She knew what she was getting into, just like we all did. So while she could not have foreseen this, we know that she would have understood.

Lila let out a small, strangled gasp, pushed her hands into her mouth to stifle it. I bowed my head. Each of us threw a handful of earth on to the partially wrapped body, the way we had seen in films.

Maybe I am not like you after all, Valerie said afterwards, when we were inside and had washed the dirt off us as best as we were able. She seemed disgusted. Maybe I am nothing like you, and the difference they spoke about exists after all. I would not make such mistakes with my freedom, so careless, so reckless. I would not be that way.

We bunched together, us blue-tickets. Fine, we said to her. Believe what you want.

Did you know that, even now, your baby is taking control of your circulatory system? Your brain, your hormones?

Lila and I shook our heads. We didn't know this. I looked to Marisol, hoping for some sign, but she gave no indication either way.

Your baby is diverting your blood supply, Valerie said. Your body is in danger but the baby will have you ignore this. The baby wants to survive at all costs, the baby doesn't care about you. It's disgusting. You think you have agency, but it's all just biology.

Don't you think you're being a little melodramatic? asked Marisol, and in her voice I heard an echo of Doctor A.

That's why you feel like you're being controlled, Valerie said, ignoring her. That's why you want to push soil into your mouth or lick salt or consume raw meat. That's the baby's way of telling you what it is missing, telling you what it needs.

Marisol sighed. Don't let her scare you, she said.

What else? I asked anyway.

The baby alters every part of you, Valerie said. There are women whose babies send them into a deep depression. There are women who are never the same again. Women who die pushing the baby out. The baby will rip your muscles and break your bones.

Marisol shook her head. It's not like that at all, she said. She made to say more, then stopped, stood and left the room.

I don't know why you want to do this. I don't know why you gave it all up, Valerie continued. All I ever wanted was freedom, all I wanted was to know that my life wasn't moving towards this dead end, but I knew it was, ever since I was twelve years old. I knew the shape of my life before I even understood what it meant.

She got to her feet, her hands in fists. I hate you in a way, she said, her face shining. I hate you all. You think the secret to happiness or whatever lies in our so-called fulfilment. You think that family fixes everything, and I will tell you now that it does not, and I'm sorry to break it to you, I'm sorry that your body has pulled such a stunt, such a dirty fucking trick, and that you can never go back. You will regret it every day of your life.

In the morning she was gone. She had taken a blanket, a sleeping bag, a bag of pasta, a box of powdered soups.

Good riddance, said Marisol. After all we did for her.

So we were back to three. Or six, depending on how you looked at it.

19

Lila stopped talking entirely after that. She spent most of her time in the tent or down by the stream. Marisol and I watched her surreptitiously from a distance to check that she would not drown herself. We followed the smudge of her as she lay on the grass, clothes rucked up so that the sunlight could reach her body. She got into the stream but it was not deep enough to do any damage.

She must have been sleepwalking, said Marisol, eyes trained upon her. Maybe she thought Therese was an emissary, in the darkness, in her sleep, and she chased her. Poor Lila. She must have thought she was an enemy. But she was wrong.

But how wrong, I wondered silently to myself. All things considered.

I thought about Valerie's parting words, and about what could happen to my body that I had not necessarily planned for. But then a lot of things had happened to my body that I had not planned.

The animal chorus came out and Marisol was distracted. Hello, my beautiful things, she said to them. But they ran away when she approached, as if we could no longer be trusted.

Stay awake, Marisol told me in the night. I get lonely.

But I couldn't; my eyes became heavy even when she pinched me hard enough to run bruises up and down my arms.

What do they do to the blue-ticket women that they catch? I asked Marisol. You know, surely?

I don't know, she said. They don't tell all of us.

You're lying, I said. I turned away from her and she didn't try to placate me, did not put her arms around me.

I'm not lying, she said. If you know one thing about me by now it's that I'm not a liar.

She was always so calm, and it killed me. Sometimes I could not bear to look at her.

They don't let you keep the baby, I assume, I said.

No, she said. You assume correctly.

Did you ever treat a white-ticket? Did you ever deliver a baby? I asked her.

No, she said. I was never allowed.

I could sense her helplessness, the frustration of knowing something, but not enough. I was not used to seeing that in her, and the vulnerability of it repelled me a little.

They must have seen it in you, I said to her, wanting to hurt her. The weakness. They knew you weren't the right sort.

Cold fish, she called me then. No longer swamp monster. No longer queen ant.

You know you can't obliterate yourself any more, she said. You've given away that right. Take your vitamins. She palmed two into my mouth and I swallowed them with no water.

But I didn't tell her that when I thought about giving birth all I saw was a tunnel of shining white light, and beyond that the purest obliteration I had ever imagined, which is to say that everything that had made me myself would fall away and then come back together, refigured, forged in the heat of a kind of love I had no comprehension of yet.

Which is to say I supposed I thought it would be like dying, but less pointless. Something to show for it.

I could hear Doctor A's response in my head as perfectly as if he stood in the room. *That's exactly the kind of thing only someone with no children would think.*

Sometimes I still wanted to ask him whether living my life on instinct was not the way I should have lived my life after all. Running, hurtling, towards the dark feeling.

A memory came back to me from the road. A raining night, dark, and I had tried to build a small shelter at the corner of a field with some tarpaulin I had found, but I was too afraid and too wet to sleep. I had heard a group of boys earlier shouting to each other as they walked, and I did not want to draw their attention. All night the mud and water ran on to me. The tarpaulin was ragged. I had stolen it from another girl when she slept, and it felt like the shame would not leave me ever, and wasn't even worth it, because it didn't do what it was supposed to. My fingers had gone white at the tips. Everything smelled rotten, even myself.

And yet. *Everything was bringing me to you*, I thought with my hands on my stomach, with something approaching surprise. *Everything, bad or good or neither, was bringing me to you all along.*

20

The safe place was no longer safe; we had been there too long, outstayed our welcome. Valerie's words filled the new silence where Therese's chatter used to be. I couldn't help but dwell on it when I woke early in the morning: Therese on the ground and the mud staining her makeshift pregnancy clothes. Even the comforting sound of the leaves had become sinister. The earth itself had turned on us.

We must remind ourselves of our purpose, said Marisol. Nobody will save us. We have to save ourselves.

We left the car where it was parked at the edge of the forest, emptied of food, and instead we walked straight on from the point of the cabin, when darkness fell. It was strange to be on the move again. My stomach had grown, and I felt weaker, as if my muscles were forgetting how to propel me. In the dark anything could be happening around us. We helped each other when we stumbled.

Morning broke and it started to rain. We pitched our tents – or rather I made up my own tent and Marisol unzipped it without asking, wriggling in next to me. We were too big to fit comfortably and I complained. She put her hand over my mouth. Hush, she said, her eyes burning out of her face, and I let her. Afterwards we fell asleep with our hands on each other's stomachs and I woke disorientated, not knowing which body was mine, which baby was mine. I had dreamed about a white room and a large egg on a table and cracking it open.

I pushed her awake. Get out, I said, I need you to get out. What's the matter? she asked, but I couldn't explain, couldn't articulate, there was a sticky fear all over me. Her hands tightened on my stomach until I prised them off. There were red marks from her fingernails on my skin.

None of us spoke as we walked onwards after sunset. Lila looked from me to Marisol from time to time, as if she wanted to ask something, then stared at the ground. The rain continued. The skin on my stomach smarted from where it had been squeezed, though the red marks had already faded to nothing.

On the second day Marisol left me alone. I slept with the knife in my hand, dipping in and out of consciousness. When we stuck our heads out into the twilight, Lila had gone. She had taken all the food. I kicked at the bare earth where her tent had been pitched.

Everybody leaves, Marisol observed, not morosely. She produced two cereal bars, one for each of us, that she had hidden in her sleeping bag. We ate them in silence.

21

We walked through the night. When we came to the edge of the forest, past dawn, we embraced, and for a second everything was back the way it was. Marisol barely showing, brushing against me in that first dark bathroom. Marisol against the pulsing broken lights of the arcade game, giving me the courage to pluck my own teeth from my gums.

We hid in the ditch at the side of the road. It was deep, enough room for us and our things. I was anxious, restless, hot prickles of electricity running over the skin of my bump. Every time a car appeared in the distance Marisol raised her head, squinted. No, she said, ducking back down. Not that one. Not that one.

Eventually a small yellow car came along. It was clean and its number plate indicated a town in the north. This one, Marisol said.

The woman driving screamed to see us moving out in front of her; our dirt-smeared faces, our bulging stomachs, our hands reaching out to tell her stop, stop, stop. It felt good to be the dangerous thing. She swerved the car and almost went off the road, but wrested it back. Marisol went up to the window. She pointed her pistol at the woman, who cringed and shut her eyes.

Wind this down, Marisol said, slamming the window with the heel of her hand. Her ruthlessness was incredible to see. It sent a shard of ice through me, both proud and ashamed.

The woman wound it down. You have to drive us somewhere, Marisol said. Open the doors, quick.

The woman pressed a button and Marisol motioned to me. In, get in, she said.

I picked up our things and opened the car door. Thank you, I said idiotically to the woman. Marisol opened the passenger door and got in next to her.

Drive, she said, and the woman did as she was told.

Marisol switched on the radio. I love this song, she said. She hummed along. I stared at the back of her head. I wondered how many Marisols were contained within her, if there was anything she could not transmit or reflect. The woman looked right ahead at the road.

Sorry about that, Marisol said, all charm again. We just needed your help. We recognized a fellow mother. We knew you'd be on our side. How many children do you have?

One, she said, not looking. Just one.

This is your family? Marisol said, pointing to a small photograph tucked into the pull-down visor on her side of the windscreen. A balding man and the woman and a small girl, with their arms around each other. They were on a beach somewhere. The girl in a red jumper, too big for her. Marisol took the photo to study it more closely and then passed it to me. The woman flinched, but didn't say anything. I studied the girl's gapped teeth, the man's smile. I felt a profound, murderous jealousy.

Marisol opened the glove compartment. I watched her do it, watched the machinations of her thoughts. The woman's papers. Her address, her name, her details. I watched her absorb the information, file it away somewhere. The woman was shaking. I could feel it where I sat, uncomfortable, in the back.

You are going to drive us where we need to go, Marisol said. You are not going to tell anybody that we were in your car. If you do, I will come for you. I will come for your child like you came for mine, like you came for hers. Do you understand?

Yes, the woman said.

We are desperate women, Marisol explained. We weren't always this way. You can understand that.

Maybe, the woman said. Her eyes met mine, briefly, in the rear-view mirror.

I like you, Marisol said, stretching out her legs, fishing out the map from her pocket. Let me show you where you're driving.

Beach

I

It was nearly dark by the time she dropped us off. We had reached the coastline, a long stretch of it pale and flat against the sky. There was a small town along its edge, sand blowing into its roads. I felt safer in the dark's blanket. Most things were shut. On the outskirts we reached a garage, neon pinks and blues, no cars at the pumps. I wanted to taste the petrol on my tongue.

Marisol spat on to a tissue and wiped dirt violently from my brow, tied back my hair so tightly that I winced. You want to look presentable, don't you? she said sternly. She waited with our packs while I went inside to buy things, feeling clean and illuminated, like the inside of my skull was hollow. My thoughts were all visible and for once they were pure. They were concentrated in my stomach. Maybe cruelty was good for the soul.

Two pints of milk, pineapple in a ring-pull can. Tiny sweet oranges in a blue net. A sliced loaf of soft white bread. Bottles of water, the cheapest they had. I missed beer, I missed cigarettes, but only in the abstract. I was a walking miracle, and alive. A man in a stained khaki apron rang all the things up for me. I felt like I could destroy him with my eyes, break his arm if he questioned my presence. Anything was possible.

If I need you to, will you cut out my baby from my body? asked Marisol as we walked towards the sea, eating bread straight from the bag. Will you make sure the baby is safe even if I am not?

Yes, I said, thinking of Therese, knowing that I would if I had to, even though gore made me feel sick, had always made me feel sick, ever since the days of my growing up.

I would cut yours from you, Marisol said.

I know, I said. That's why I didn't ask.

In the dunes we pitched just one tent. Easier to hide, Marisol said, and I had to agree that mine was too conspicuous, the red flag of it stuffed deep in my backpack. The moon was bright and liverish. I sat with my body inside and my legs outside, folded up, watching the line of Marisol's throat as she tipped her pint of milk up to the sky and drained it. Her mouth was pink and wet.

I went for a walk alone across the beach, asking Marisol to stay behind. Her eyes were on me as I made my way down the sand dunes, almost falling, not quite. My hair became loose and was blown into my eyes, grit against my mouth and I swallowed it, taking in the ocean. Out over the grey line of the sea, the sky was peach and crossed with lines of light.

Along the shoreline, the sand was wet and packed. When I looked down at my feet I couldn't see them past my stomach, but I could see my footprints behind me, as if they were something independent, a ghost following my trail. I started to laugh at nothing, leaned over, my hands flat on my knees. In my pockets I put seaweed, shell, a piece of wood worn bone-smooth. When I looked back I was further than I'd realized and Marisol was a speck on the dunes, too far away to see if she were raising an arm to me. The horizon was golden, and where she sat was dark. I could have walked into the sea or just kept going on that sand, on and on following the coastline where it snaked around, but instead I started to return. Return was possible. The pockets of my jacket were full. They smacked against my body as I walked.

2

By dawn, the tent was milky with breath, strewn with pieces of orange peel. When she woke, Marisol's eyes were swollen. My heart, she said, does it feel strange to you? I took her pulse and then pressed my hand to the left side of her chest. It was slightly faster than it should have been. I know too much about what can go wrong with bodies, she said.

We ate more oranges and slices of the packaged bread, but we were still hungry afterwards. Our appetites were raging, the babies telling us that they were almost ready. We stink, Marisol said balefully. Well, let's go in the sea then, I replied, but she shook her head, listed the dangers. Rip tides, weevers, jellyfish.

We buried our evidence, fruit peels and the plastic wrapping of the bread pressed loosely into the sand. The sea had come much closer to us. As we walked along the beach, we stayed near to the dunes. I took off my jacket. The sun hit my skin, warmed it.

What's wrong with you? I asked her.

She didn't reply right away.

Some animals bury themselves in the ground when they give birth, she said eventually. Some animals leave their eggs in the sand. And others leave the baby alone to fend for itself. Did you know that a human child can't look after itself for the first five years of its life?

That's a long time, I said.

It's what you signed up for, she said. And the rest of it.

She walked behind me. My neck prickled. Neither of us moved to touch, to hold the other's hand.

Some mothers eat their young, she said. And others, the true mothers, are consumed by the children they produce. Spiders do it. They allow their offspring to swarm. They see themselves for what they are, which is sustenance. Meat.

We walked for a while longer. Why do you have to be so morbid, I wanted to ask. Why can't you be happy that we got this far.

When we pitched the tent once more I could not sleep. Marisol was snoring lightly. It was lovely to watch her, despite everything. To see the flex of her toes as they moved in her dreams. But I was too restless to settle, so I crawled outside to where my rucksack was set beside hers, expectant. I found myself picking it up, heaving it on to my shoulders. It seemed a little less heavy than before, or maybe I was just used to the weight. Motion seemed important, suddenly. I decided to go for a walk.

I hadn't got very far before I felt a loosening, an unslinging. In the base of my stomach, something was pulling or being pulled. A sharpness rushing and receding, like the tide, and in that moment of pain something opening me up, up and away. My legs were wet. Marisol had told me that when the baby was coming, the water it lived in would be released first. The small ocean in which the baby swam. The wide ocean behind me. I watched the sand dampen around my feet.

All right, I said. All right.

I didn't turn back.

3

Sand gave way to a group of small houses, yellow-painted. Flowers and shells in the gardens, benches on which you could sit and breathe in the sea air. White-ticket. Looking in the windows was irresistible, looking in at the life I had been found unworthy of. Loving, and being loved. It made my heart beat quickly and bile rise in my throat. I wanted to transport myself to R's future, to his own white-ticket home and his own fat baby in a pram, and push my face against his glass window, to hurt myself with it. The pain was good, distracted me from the other pain rippling through my body, periodically, building in tandem with my fear. I remembered the woman in the film, her mouth stretched open, the classical music masking her noises.

There was nobody awake in the first house, lights off as I tried to make out details – furnishings, ornaments, the colour of the walls. Same at the second, the third. It was the fourth house where I struck gold. A window at the back with one lamp lit. It was the kitchen, and inside it was a woman. There was no need to see her locket. She held a baby in her arms, nakedly vulnerable without the protection of the pram. The sight took my breath away. The baby waved a small hand towards her face, caught her lip and pulled it down. The woman kissed the top of the baby's head and opened the fridge, searching for something. I cried a few hard tears, involuntarily, as if I had been punched, and then I pulled myself together.

It was easy to pick the lock. When I let myself into the house, I pretended for a second that it was my own, that I was returning to what was rightfully mine. Look: the warm wood of the floorboards, the table on which the telephone sits. I left my rucksack next to the coat rack, setting it down silently. I would have decorated differently, would have stripped the wallpaper and painted the floor. I was full of anger. This should have been mine. What had I done to be excluded? What was wrong with me? It was the question I had been asking my whole life. I stopped, crouched to the floor as the pain went through me again, hot and unfamiliar. I breathed, waited, stood. I went towards the kitchen. The woman was facing away from me, seated and holding the baby to her body. I put a hand on her mouth from behind her, wrapped my other arm around her waist, and she stiffened but could not fight me, not with the child in her arms. If anyone had seen us it would have looked as though we were locked in an embrace.

Don't scream, don't scream, I whispered to her, my mouth at her ear. Her hair smelled of honey and fresh linen. She juddered under my hands, tried to crane around and my bump pressed against her harder. I don't want to hurt you, I promise.

The knife was still in the hand of my arm that was restraining her. I leaned forward and put it on the table, where she could see it, and she went limp.

I don't want to hurt you, I repeated. But I need you to be quiet. Will you be quiet?

She nodded. I waited a few seconds, then let my hand drop. She stood up and immediately moved to the other side of the table. Her blouse was open. The baby stirred against her.

Please don't take my baby, she said, her voice low and dark. Please, I'll give you anything, just don't take my baby.

I don't want your baby, I said, and I pressed my hands to the swell of my stomach so she could see it properly. I'm like you, I said, even though it was clear I was not, and the obviousness of this filled me with a wounding shame.

Why are you here? the mother said. The baby began to fuss, picking up on the tension. Oh sweet, oh beautiful, she said to the baby, the soft language of it almost unknown to me, bringing me to tears again. I wiped them away angrily, picked up the knife.

I want to know what to do, I said. Something's happening to me.

She was looking at the baby, not me. I don't know what to tell you, she said. I don't know where to begin.

Please, I said. Another bolt of pain. I closed my eyes, breathed through my teeth, and when I opened them she was looking at me, at the wet patch on my dress, at my juddering chest.

Oh, she said.

I sat down on a chair and motioned with the knife for her to do the same, even though it was her house. She sat at the other end of the table, heavily.

Start from the beginning, I said. Start with the basics.

Her eyes were wide. You're in labour, she said. The pain will get worse and worse. And then. She hesitated.

And then what? I asked. Quickly, please.

Well, and then you push the baby out. She motioned vaguely. The baby will come out on a cord, and you have to cut the cord, but not too soon. You have to wait until the placenta comes out, that's the red thing on the end, there's no mistaking it when it comes.

It was like she was speaking another language. The baby started to move against her blouse and she turned away from me slightly as she did something, gave the baby access to her body. She turned back and I realized that the baby was attached to her nipple, its mouth locked on to her flesh. I thought about the heaviness of my breasts, hard and blue when I undressed, and it made a terrible new sense.

Her eyes were shadowed under the light of the overhead lamp.

You'll watch the baby every second of the day. You'll be convinced they're dying. You'll hold them to your body and weep. Sometimes you will think of killing them yourself.

I put the knife down.

You're not a white-ticket, she said to me. It wasn't a question. I don't think you really understand what you've done. What kind of trouble you're in.

I can cope with trouble, I said.

I don't mean the emissaries, though they will surely find you, she said. I mean the other trouble, the motherhood trouble. The trouble that doesn't leave you.

She touched her baby's head very lightly. Come with me, she said. Let's put him to sleep.

I followed her up the stairs, knife in my pocket. She whispered into her child's ear, the soft language again. Together we went into a room lit dimly amber. Stand in the corner, she said to me, growing braver. Stand with your hands visible.

I chose to trust her. My palms, displayed nakedly to her, were hard and sheened with sweat. Life line, heart line, sun line. Old magic from the countryside, the other girls holding my hands in theirs, predicting things.

This is how you lay a baby down, she told me. With exaggerated slowness she placed the child on its back. Do not put the baby on their side, she said, with sudden vehemence. The baby could die if they are left on their side. This is important to remember. Nobody will tell you this but I'm telling you now.

The baby put a foot into its own mouth, athletically.

This is how you wrap a baby, she told me, pulling a blanket over it, making sure its arms were free. This is how you make sure the baby does not get too hot. Babies cannot control their temperature. They cannot regulate their emotions. They are wholly dependent on you. They are terrifying, even I can admit that.

She touched the baby's bald head again and then set the mobile spinning, shadows dancing on the wall.

What if you didn't want it? I asked, as I watched the baby release its foot from the blanket and wriggle. What if you couldn't?

I wanted it, she said. I don't know about anyone else. I don't want to know.

I hesitated. Do you know what happens to the blue-ticket mothers that are caught?

No, she said. How should I know?

We left the baby's room and she moved silently to another, a bedroom where her husband was sleeping. I watched him from the doorway. He made no noise, not even breathing. He seemed dead. I wished him dead. I wished them a fracture in their happy life. The woman opened her wardrobe and found some garments, handed them to me word-lessly. She lifted a finger to her lips. The husband turned over but did not wake.

I have not slept a full night in months, the woman told me, in the hall. I long to sleep the sleep of the fathers.

Help me, I asked her. Please help me.

She shook her head.

No, no, she said. Her shoulders hunched up to her ears. You really have to go now. I've done too much. More than you deserve.

I left the house, and outside I held up what she had given me to the light of a streetlamp. A blue blanket, a pink flowered dress. I looked back once more towards the house. In her pool of golden light, pro-tected light, I saw her lift up a telephone and press the numbers one by one. She looked out of the window and made eye contact with me, then turned away.

The pain was everywhere. I started to walk, and then I started to run. It was harder once I reached the sand, but I knew I could do it. I knew there was no other choice.

4

I was alone again and it felt right. The word *abandoning* came into my head, the image of Marisol's face when she discovered me gone, but I couldn't really think about it, I was busy with the pain, with forward motion. Something had clicked into place. The feeling was leading me somewhere, down the beach, skirting the edge of the dunes, searching for safety.

Above me, just beyond my eyeline, a staircase; a small box of light. They used to peel the martyrs of their skin. A woman in a bar had told me that one night, at the stage of being drunk when the universe starts to reveal things. They used to say that transcendence was something more than bodily. If you're attached to your body you can't get anywhere.

Said who? I'd asked at the time. Who are *they*? And what do they know about my body?

Soon, blue morning, a sky washed with light. I felt cold. I looked down at my stomach, and there it was, undeniable. The sand gathered around my feet like snow.

No more houses, no more mothers and fathers. The occasional sound of a loud car on some road parallel, very far away.

As I walked, I wondered about sly Valerie and her black eye. I wondered about the old woman in the bed and breakfast, and the woman I had seen at the swimming pool, serene in her childlessness the way you could be serene in your motherliness. They were a chorus, asking me, What do you even want it for?

I don't know, I told them. I've got this far and I still don't know. But I think I am finding peace in that, regardless.

On a large piece of driftwood I sat for a second. I smoothed my thoughts. Lichen and barnacles were already colonizing this thing that had been a tree for many years. The sea had taken it in and spat it out, made it new. It occurred to me that it was not too late to just go in and swim for a while.

The baby kicked inside me. Don't be morbid, they were saying. Anyway, you've already annihilated your life. If you want to look at it that way.

To pathologize desire into flat compulsion reduces the possibilities of it. Which is not to say that I had not felt compulsion. But perhaps I was learning the difference, finally, between that and conviction. Between something enacted in the name of desperation, and something enacted in the name of curiosity. In the name of beauty. In the name of a sort of love.

Call it maternal instinct. Call it accepting the impermanence of all things. Call it kindness, finally, shown towards myself.

All right, I said to my baby. To my body. Just another part of the conversation we had been having my whole life. My body that was mine, and belonged to me, and always had.

My child, waiting for me with endless patience. Not knowing the person I had been. Only the person I could become.

I got to my feet.

5

There was only so far that I could go. The parameters of my body and what it could do were narrowing down to a sharp point. I went into the dunes again, pulled out the red tent. No one to see it here. No choice even if they could.

There was no position right for my body any more, no good way to place it. In the end I got on all fours and let my belly hang to the ground. I leaned my face on to sand and it stuck to my wet cheek. I let myself make noises that I would never have made otherwise.

Pain scrunched me up, tiny and ineffectual. Then it opened me up at the ribs, the pelvis, like I was being disarticulated on a butcher's block. Then it was a horse bolting away from me. It was impossible to get a grip on it.

Soft body learning to be hard on the country roads. Gravel; wet, steaming air in my nostrils. Body of tarmac and hotel rooms and swimming pools and bathrooms and clinics, body of ripped-up cuticles and appetite and sex with people loved and not-loved, a body forgiving every bad thing I could do to it. A body always going somewhere. Carrying me onwards. Never letting me down, yet.

I thought of the border as a clear line between old life and new. I thought of it as an illuminated mark on the ground. You could step over and back. You could be in two places at the same time.

Okay, I told myself. I peeled off my dress, my underwear, all of it ruined anyway. Sweat made my skin slick. My hands were shaking. I knelt like I was praying, I braced. I went up the ladder of the pain, rung by rung, until I was a long way above the ground. Until I was a long way above myself.

In my head there was a shining white road and there were no cars approaching, and I lay down on it, and it was not gravel, it was smooth marble, and I waited for whatever was going to run me over to run me over. For whatever was going to peel me back up to peel me back up.

Give yourself over to it, I told myself, the way I had told myself before in my old life, over and over, for every bad decision, every bad feeling, maybe I had been practising all those years, maybe I had been preparing myself without knowing. *Surrender.*

Through everything I saw desire dimly in the distance like a sheet of rain, and it was infinite, refracted many ways. I was astonished and moved at the possibilities it held. How it had got me here.

Deep pressure. I pushed, and nothing seemed to happen, but the urge to push didn't stop and neither did I, it was the only thing my body was capable of. My breathing was ragged, sobbing. I put my hand between my legs and touched something solid.

Baby. Strange and full of life. She came out in a hot, tumbling way. I caught her in my hands. She was blue and then she was screaming — companion noise to my own, I realized, two parts in the same orchestra, playing from a single sheet. My body was still doing things. I was bleeding and then I was pushing something else out. Lung-like thing on a rope, pain's aftershock racking my body. *Surrender.* The baby was still screaming but her skin changed from purple to red. Alien sea-creature. *Surrender.* I didn't know if I loved her from the first second, I was too afraid to make those sorts of value judgements, but I knew that I would die for her, and that was more important. *Surrender.* I held my daughter. I pressed her skin against mine.

6

The sun was high in the sky. We watched each other with some fear, but even I could tell that I was the one more afraid. I held her tiny hand between my thumb and forefinger, very gingerly. Her palm was little bigger than a fingerprint. She was still marbled with fat and blood, glossy, like a steak just unwrapped from its paper. A little sand stuck to her. Facts came back to me: water in my plastic bottle, tepid. The cord, which needed to be cut off, like the woman had told me. I had no idea how to do it, was afraid to use my dirty knife, so in the end I tucked the strange, fleshy bag into the blanket alongside her. I quickly became used to the gore everywhere.

Nova was the name I had chosen in the forest, the name foraged from scraps, from things written and remembered and listed. I had picked it and never told anyone. The secret was out. I told my daughter her own name. Nova was a puckered thing, mottled, feathered on top with dark hair. She was unbelievably strange. I never wanted to be apart from her again.

When she started to cry I put her on my chest, copying what I had seen. Come on, I told her. Eat something. Her mouth opened and closed. I had the idea she might take small bites from my flesh, leave tiny wounds, and I would welcome it, I would tell her to take whatever she needed. I needed to wash but had no idea how I was supposed to do that while carrying her. In the end I just pulled the dress the woman had given me over my bloodstained body, reasoning it was better than nothing.

We slept in fragments. My whole body hurt. I didn't know how to make the pain go away. Sometimes I stuck my head out of the tent to measure the progress from light to dark and back again. With my hands and eyes I scoped out the damage. I had been lucky, it seemed, to escape the physical catastrophes that Valerie had warned us about, though maybe they were yet to come, or maybe my brain was loosening in my skull even as I examined myself, and soon I'd walk us both into the ocean. The minute I thought about it I told myself to stop, but doing that made it impossible. To distract myself, I watched Nova sleeping, and then I slept myself.

When I woke up, the light was filtering through the canvas, turning everything red. Nova's face glowed. I lay still and listened, holding my baby tight to me. Shh, I whispered to her.

There was movement; someone passed the tent, and then someone else. Voices too quiet to make out what they were saying. The zip of the tent started to move down. I watched it, reached for the knife.

The face of a woman that I didn't know. She was pale and impassive as the moon. It's over, she said. Get out.

I screamed at her — all my anger, all my fear, all of everything I had been storing up for the last days and months and years — but she did not react. She blinked one long, calm blink. Then I was pulled from the tent by decisive hands, my body protesting, still in pain. My mind went to the knife but in the confusion I was afraid of hurting Nova, so I let it fall and concentrated on cupping my hands around her instead. The baby has come already? I heard someone exclaim. Someone check the baby! Hands reached for Nova but I screamed again and they dropped away from her soft body, came back to mine. Nova's screaming joined my own, the siren of her voice making my heart surge. Men and women dressed in navy. They didn't speak to me, just led the two of us inland through the dunes until we came to their glossy cars, parked on the road beyond the beach.

Beside the cars was a man in a long white coat. It was Doctor A. He waved from a distance away. Morning, he said when we were close enough to hear him. You did pretty well. He raised his eyebrows at Nova in my arms. I hope it was worth it, he said.

I had a vision of myself kneeling on the floor and Doctor A as an executioner, coming towards me wearing a hood. Seeing him outside of the clinic felt wrong. He looked relaxed, jovial even. I wanted him to put his arms around me and tell me it was all a mistake.

He opened the door of a gleaming red car with a white interior. It smelled like bleach and leather. I sat in the back with Nova in my arms. The locks of the doors clicked immediately behind us. Hanging from the rear-view mirror was an air freshener the shape of an opening rose. A bag of striped peppermints in the tray behind the gearstick. Want one? Doctor A asked. When I shook my head he put one into his mouth and started the car.

His eyes met mine in the mirror. He seemed younger, almost my age. He paused to light up a cigarette, did not roll down the window. I had never seen him smoke before. Somehow it changed everything.

So, he exhaled. Here we are.

Border

I

He drove us a short distance to a long, flat, brick building, similar to the lottery station all those years ago. Perhaps I would always end up in the same places, regardless of how far I ran. The emissaries had followed us in their cars, pulling up one by one and getting out briskly, while we sat in silence, apparently waiting for something.

I've taken a special interest, he said, as though he could read my mind, which possibly he could. You just never seemed maternal at all, so, professionally, it's quite irregular.

He twisted around, reached one slightly damp hand to my bare forearm. Fingers circling my wrist. Besides, we've been through so much together.

Out of the car, he led me inside alone, through empty white corridors to a sparse room with windows overlooking the sea, a single bed with pink sheets and a lacy valance. He sat on the bed and gestured for me to do the same.

I remember what my son was like at this age. Looking at a newborn always brings it back to me. May I?

He was already reaching for her, prising her out of my arms. He handled her like someone who was used to babies. A father after all, a white-ticket woman at home. Nova started to cry.

Oh, I didn't mean to set her off, he said. Babies, you know. Well, actually, I suppose you don't.

He laughed a little. Nudged my knee with his, as if I were in on the joke.

I was very tired. I wanted to kill him. I would murder him and eat of him. I would daub Nova in his blood. I hated watching her in his large, beautiful hands. I hated thinking of him as a father. I hated thinking of him throwing balls in the garden or putting children to bed.

Nova was still crying and my dress was wet with milk. It was terrible. I cried then too, from the humiliation. To be an animal in front of him. I was turned inside out and there was nothing that would put me back the way I had been, I would be wet and alien for all time, skinned.

It's interesting for me to see you like this, he said.

I wanted to hide my face, but instead I made myself stare back at him.

I need to examine you both, he said, putting Nova down on the bed.

He unpacked his kit – the inflatable orange band, the vials for my blood, the spirometer. After so long without a check-up there was a hint of the occult to those objects. I capitulated, mindful of the changes my body had gone through. I breathed out as hard as I could when instructed, I lay down on the bed with my legs apart, I let the signs of my body be translated. My thighs were smeared with blood, still, down to the knee. He dabbed at my skin with gauze, antiseptic, water, then when I was cleaned up he pushed his latex hands inside me. Only a couple of stitches, he said from between my legs. You're a little torn. I felt him piece my skin back together, sharp pain, then something different. Don't move, he said. An object scraping inside me, the little wishbone of wire. My body tensed. No, no, I said.

You want to move, I can tell, he said, but if you move you'll do yourself some real damage.

So I lay still. When he was done he handed me a tissue and I realized I was crying. He reached into his briefcase and withdrew a syringe.

Antibiotics, he said. In case you caught something nasty on the road. You want to stay well for your baby, don't you? Arm out, please.

No, I said, wresting myself away. I don't want that.

Honestly, Calla. You don't have a choice. He took up my arm again. I shut my eyes. My veins were small, but the needle slid in with ease. Almost immediately I felt fogged, heavier. I watched stupidly as he picked up Nova again. Put her down, put her down, I said. I tried to stand but it was difficult; I listed sideways and back on to the bed.

Sleep, he said, turning with her in his arms. When you've rested you can have a nice hot shower, wash all that mess off you properly.

Panic grew in me. He was not putting her down, he was walking out of the door, but I was already falling, the adrenaline in my body fading to nothing.

In the night I awoke alone. I banged on the door and shouted for her, but nobody came. I tried the windows, I pulled everything off the bed and checked underneath it, and then I put my face into the pillow and howled. My stomach, still swollen, was the only proof she had ever existed. The pain still in my body.

The room had an en-suite and eventually I staggered into it. It hurt to pee, my feet splayed on the yellowed tiles. Dying carnations in a flower arrangement next to the mirror. I was tired of the dressing-up of death and ugliness and all the rest of it. I thought I could hear a baby crying from somewhere, very faint, but perhaps it was the whine of the lightbulb in its electrical socket, perhaps it was the air conditioning. My body knew it wasn't Nova. I had to believe that, to believe my body telling me it was not my child crying in a locked room without me. I couldn't allow myself to fall apart. I had to be a knife. I had to find a way out and back to her.

The next day Doctor A came back. I wished not to be glad to see him. He took me to a different room. There were two chairs padded with red vinyl, a small square table, a counter with a hot plate and a pot of brewing coffee, with biscuits laid out neatly in rows. The room was long and the furniture only took up the first third, with space yawning behind us, as if for an audience. I could imagine more chairs set up, a conference on my badness taking place, my fate decided.

My grief pulled me underwater once again. Nova.

Where is she? I asked Doctor A, but he acted as though he had not heard me. He took the further chair, his legs spread wide open, and I sat down opposite him. Leaning forward, he pulled the table to one side, so that there was nothing in between us. It seemed to take him no effort at all and this worried me. I was pulling in information from my surroundings, anything that could be of use. Beautiful day, he said, looking outside.

On the table lay a long, black hair. I stared at it, wondering who it belonged to. Doctor A watched me with a detached interest. I wondered if he could still predict my behaviour, if there was a pattern women like me repeated. I wondered how many women had sat at this table with him.

Without the flat weight of Nova attached to me, I felt lopsided already. That was how it worked, when something had been cleaved from your body. I was crying openly but silently. What else could my body be doing but that – the pouring of water, the shock of the separation.

I wanted my baby. I wanted the white ticket and all it represented in my hand. I wanted to have been a bundle of hair and cloth in the back of a car all along, carried to safety. I wanted maternal instinct to have shone from me, infallible, undeniable, like a light. I would have done the unspeakable for her. Wasn't that proof of something? I could see in the way Doctor A watched me that it was unbecoming to see someone like me have such feelings, like watching a dog taught to speak.

Get a handle on yourself, he told me, with faint disgust.

He walked to where the coffee was brewing and brought back two full cups and a jug of cream on a tray.

You can drink this now, he said, handing one to me. It's safe for you again.

I didn't touch it. There was stuffing leaking out from my seat and my fingers tangled in it. There was the blue sea, still, in my eyeline, out of the window.

Where is she? I asked again.

Doctor A set his cup down. You might be interested to know that another woman lives in your house now. She walked into the city and into that life. She's grateful for the freedom it allows, in a way that you weren't. She goes to her doctor like you came to me. She wears her locket and believes in it.

In another life, as he carried on explaining to me, I had grown tired of R. I had carried on with my work. I had met a person I cared for, who cared for me too, and we had made a home. Not a white-ticket home, but a home.

Or I had never met anyone I loved enough to settle down with, but I was fine with it. I made a different sort of home. I travelled, I had exciting affairs. I died alone and old and glad in my bed.

You could have been happy that way, Doctor A said.

But I would have had to live with the dark feeling every day, I said, my voice hard. Heavy in my stomach. Thinking of it always.

Yes, Doctor A agreed. You would have carried it around. Maybe one day it would have dissolved. You would have forgotten it.

But I wouldn't have.

Well, he said. No guarantee.

It would have got worse, I said. It would have choked off everything.

Maybe, he said. Maybe it would have got worse.

It doesn't matter any more. All that matters is Nova. I stood up, but he waved me back down with his hand. Don't overexert yourself, he said.

He carried on talking about pointless things, about R in his high, clean apartment – how sometimes in the evening he poured whisky into a thick glass and walked around after three of these glasses or so, not going anywhere. There was a white-ticket woman, I had been right. It might have been my fault that there was. I might have put the idea in him.

He'll have a baby and he'll push it around in a big pram, Doctor A said. It just won't be yours.

There was no cruelty in his tone. There didn't need to be. He was just relating a fact.

What will happen to Nova? Is she all right? I asked. There was nothing else I could think about.

He sighed. You have to realize that Nova does not exist any more. You won't see her again. She'll be given to someone suitable, a real family, a real mother. One day she'll pick her own ticket at the lottery. It's too early to say what colour it will be, of course. I don't know that yet. You never will.

I laughed and it sounded like choking. It did not seem possible that we would never know each other, when we were already intertwined enough that her pain was my pain, that her cries summoned my milk, made me frantic with her need. I shut my eyes, opened them again, trying to reset the scene, to wipe it clean.

Doctor A got up abruptly, walked to the other end of the room. Let me give you a minute, he said. He put his hands on the windowsill, gazing outside.

She was gone. I had failed. I thought about what I could have done differently. About keeping myself alone, speaking to nobody, no hotels, no men in those hotels, no Marisol, no women dead on the ground. I thought about the survival pack they had given me, the red tent and the map that was wrong and the gun almost too heavy for my hands. Those cruel objects saying to me: Go on then. Prove how much you want it, if you really do want it so much. A little joke. A little mercy. What was it all for, if not to teach us what it means to survive, what it means to push, what it means to love?

What about earning it? I said aloud. You said. You said I could prove that I was good enough.

Doctor A looked across to me. No, Calla, he said. Nobody told you that.

He came back and sat down again in the same chair. He leaned in closer to me.

You're not meant to like your patients, but sometimes you can't help it, he said. You ferry them along through each crisis. You know their lives better than your own. You hold their pain, teach them to reshape it. Sometimes the pain is too big.

Fuck you, I said.

I wish I could have helped you, he said.

You could help me now, I said.

No, I can't.

Fuck you, I said again.

That doesn't help anyone, does it, he said. Tell me that you understand what's going to happen. That you accept it, that you give yourself over to it.

I told him instead that I'd had agency over the things I had done all through my life, even if not over everything that had been done to me. I told him I was not a branch being broken in a stream, carried along by the water until it snapped. I told him he should give my baby back to me. I told him that some things couldn't be seen in a person, that mistakes could be made, that there was no quantifying what made a true mother. I told him that he should give my baby back to me. I told him that having seen badness, having known badness and even at times been badness, I felt only the more compelled to keep my baby from it. That I couldn't do anything about whatever crucial lack was inside myself – whatever had been seen or decided, sniffed out from my body or my brain or my soul – but I could do this.

Give my baby back to me, I said again.

He leaned forwards, took my twisting hands in his, and my whole body tensed.

I'm going to tell you the truth, because I respect you, he said. You weren't given a blue ticket because of anything you did or anything you are. It was random. It could have happened to any of you. There's no deserving. There is no order – at least not one that governs the lottery. There's a yes and a no, and that's all. And yet see how it became true, see how you fulfilled your destiny, how you even relished the blue, at first? Don't interrupt me. I know that you were happy for quite some time. But you couldn't accept it; you thought you were better than what you were given.

So I could have been a white-ticket all along, I said.

And you probably wouldn't have been happy with that either, he said. You've always wanted more.

I couldn't argue with that. I didn't have the energy to even try. What are they going to do to me? I asked instead.

He smiled. He looked tired too, suddenly. It's over, Calla, he said. They're not going to do anything. Try to relax.

I don't understand.

Haven't you remembered what it's like to be cold, alone, in danger? he said. Don't you feel you've been punished enough? But it's all right. You'll be taken to a new city and given another chance to make your own life. Try to appreciate it this time.

I thought about the weeks on the road, believing that Nova and I could make it, that the life we wanted was out there ahead of us. The quiet green of the months in the cabin, my daughter growing inside me, every day alive. My punishment. Doctor A's face hovered in front of me, oblivious. How could he not know that that punishment had been the best and truest part of my life? Possibly I was not the sort of person who should be a mother, but I had heard what was calling through my body and I chose the burden of it. I chose freedom, even if to some it looked like the opposite.

He released my hands, shuffled his chair slightly closer to me. I always liked talking to you, he said. It's all such a shame. I thought you had potential. Sometimes I made admiring notes.

This seemed so ridiculous that I started to laugh, which turned into crying again. I wanted to lie down. I was so weary.

Do you have any final requests, while we're here? he asked. He paused, meaningfully. You haven't asked about the girl you were with.

Marisol, I said. My mouth was dry, the name unfamiliar. Eyes sore. I didn't want to know how he knew about her.

She's a doctor, as you know, Doctor A said. Or she was. Quite a senior one, as it happens. And she made a bargain with us. He looked at me expectantly.

What sort of bargain? I asked. I hated having to ask, to beg for the information. She persuaded them to let her go?

I know this is difficult to hear, he said.

It's not, I lied reflexively. He raised his eyebrows.

Fine. She had been doing good work before she got pregnant, and she sensibly decided to carry on doing that work. She would find fugitive women on the road and deliver them to us – gaining their trust and leading them to places where they would be picked up. She was extremely good at it, as we knew she would be. Just a few months' service. In return, she could keep her own baby, and the two of them could leave the country.

I thought about the first woman I had seen with her, their heads pressed close, formulating a plan. About Marisol driving her to a dark place where the emissaries waited and then driving on again, in a new car, the woman left behind.

She trapped me, I said.

She almost didn't, he said. She went off the grid for a long time after she met you. We were curious about whether she had done something stupid. Out of character, for her. But in the end she came back to us, as we knew she would. She put her baby first.

He reached for my hands again and held them tighter than before, so tightly that the bones shifted.

You made it easy, in the end, for her to betray you, he said. That's always been the sort of person you are. Even without your ticket, that was obvious in you from the start.

The feel of my hands in his was the worst thing. I would rather have had his around my neck. Rosary of bruises, half-moon marks from his nails. The kindness was worse than the cruelty. There was genuine compassion in his eyes. Perhaps he would cry. I kept watching. He let go of my hands. He didn't cry.

2

An emissary led me back to the room with the bed. She was small, blonde, chewed gum when she thought I wasn't looking. I imagined overpowering her, seizing her gun and bringing the butt of it down on to her face. But my breasts were leaking, the skin tight as a drum and painful. I had to go at once to the bathroom and massage them, and watched with a sort of muted horror as milk fell from me into the toilet bowl, relieving some of the pressure. Then I sat on the bed in a circle of lamplight and waited for something. I counted to a hundred and then a thousand, and then counted backwards, emptying my thoughts, let the static of that monotony fill the air, but it didn't work. I knew there should have been a sort of comfort in knowing, finally, that there had been nothing missing in me – nothing seen or judged, as I had been made to believe my whole life – but the comfort was abstract, cold, out of reach.

I stayed in the room a long time before a knock came at the door. I pressed my eye eagerly to the tiny fishbowl lens but it was not Nova. It was Marisol. She was not staring back at me but looking at the floor, looking down the corridor. I stepped back from the door, sick, as she let herself in. She was dressed in the white coat of the doctors. She looked exactly how I had imagined: her hair pulled back, smooth. There was no baby with her, not mine and not hers. She carried a tray holding a foil-covered plate, two glasses of water, a packet of cigarettes.

Hello, she said.

Do you know where she is? I almost shouted it.

Good to see you too, she said. She drained her glass of water, but I would not take mine when she offered it.

Tell me, I said.

She sat on the end of the bed. There was nowhere else to sit. She perched decorously, stiffly, legs crossed at the ankle, and laid the tray on the ground in front of her.

Do you mind if I smoke? she asked.

Yes, I said, but she lit one anyway.

I watched her closely, trying to see the motherliness in her. She seemed very remote, though I knew objectively that I had touched her, that I had cared for her. I wanted to put my hands around her neck until she gave me answers. An echo of love, of anger, passed over me and then left.

Where's my baby? I asked again. Where's yours?

She blew smoke out, tilting her head away from me. Sleeping, she said. Another room.

She unfolded the cover from the plate to reveal crustless sandwiches, stubbed the cigarette out on the crumpled foil.

Want one? she said, offering it to me.

What the fuck is wrong with you? I asked.

I'm hungry, she said. You know what that feels like, I know you do. You're the hungriest person I've ever met.

She put the plate down, didn't take one herself after all.

Marisol. Why are you here?

You want to see your baby, don't you? she said. Come with me. I'm going to help you.

We walked down the corridor together. There was nobody else there now. Marisol seemed at home in this place where nothing should have been at home. She moved decisively, gracefully. I hated her. She paused at a large wooden door, took a key from her pocket, put it in the lock and turned.

The room was painted yellow, like the walls of the halfway house all those years ago. Muslin was draped from the windows and over the wooden cots lined up against the far wall. There were five cots, and only one baby. At once I knew her, even swaddled in new white cloth. She was wrapped in a complicated way, but her arms were free. I took her up and Marisol hung back, leaving me alone.

The nurse is on her break, she said, staring at the wall.

Nova in my arms was warm and delicious as a loaf of bread. Dopamine rushed my brain, dulled me, softened my edges. In my peripheral vision, Marisol fidgeted uneasily, half stepping towards us then glancing back at the door.

Where's yours? I asked.

Not here, obviously. Marisol smiled. Let's sit down for a minute.

What? No. We have to get her out of here, now, before someone comes.

Marisol shook her head. It's not safe yet. We have to wait.

We sat together on the floor, between two cots. The only light came from a rabbit-shaped nightlight plugged into the wall socket, casting a gold blush. Nova was sprawled against my chest like a frog. The rhythm of my breathing seemed to soothe her.

Do you remember the first time we saw each other? Marisol asked.

Yes, I said. I was afraid of you.

It might have been better if we had never met, she said.

Better is relative, I said. It would have been different.

I saw another journey, one where I had been very alone, one that had ended sooner, before I had a chance to meet Nova. Ended on the side of the road, or in the hotel with the man who hit me, or asleep in a bathtub, or pulled over by the authorities. I also saw a journey where I had made it, where I had been once more the girl with the scratched knees, ruthless, a thing of the dark. Where I had tunnelled through dirt and swum and stolen and hurt my way to freedom.

I was afraid of you too, she said. I was afraid of everyone.

Well, you didn't seem it, I said.

You can't let anyone see that you are, or it will all be over, she said. You have to just pretend. But I'm still afraid. I am more afraid than ever. I can tell you now, because it doesn't matter.

It does matter, and I'm not afraid, I said, but didn't know if it was true. Maybe I could be the brave one, for once. I knew that the dark feeling no longer seemed dark, that it was glowing, that I had seen and even touched the hot wet redness of the universe, but I didn't want to talk about that with Marisol, even though she was a mother now too.

Good for you, she said. Can I hold her?

No, I said. I can't forgive you, you know. Even by giving her back to me. You betrayed us.

Only at the end, she said. Only when I had to. I betrayed others, that's true. I did terrible things so that I could keep my baby. But the woods, and us, that was real. She shifted, looked away. But you left, and my baby was not moving, and I had to go back to them. I needed help, it was an emergency, and you had abandoned me. Of course, once I was there I had to tell them about you. Of course I did. I had to keep my end of the bargain. She looked up and her eyes were hard and wet. I don't care whether you understand it or not. I know you would have done the same thing.

Her gaze dropped to Nova's face, she reached out to touch her cheek with one finger. I moved my daughter closer to my body, away.

But it was no good anyway, she said. I have no baby.

I looked away from Nova and into Marisol's eyes, properly, for the first time since we had entered the room, and the air went cold around me.

He was a boy, she said. He hadn't been moving for a while. I was right, but I hadn't wanted to believe it. He was born without a heart-beat. I held him in my arms but I knew right away, how could I not? So I no longer have a baby.

She gave a sharp, sobbing laugh. She made to take Nova, but I kept my arms tight around her.

I have no baby, but I can leave this country, I can do it honestly, I can make a life, she said. I've earned it. They don't care whose baby I take.

No, I said. Don't ask me. Don't say it.

Marisol bared her teeth. I had never seen her like this before. She was crying openly.

Give me your baby, she said. Give me your baby and I promise that I will care for her as my own. I promise that she will be happy and loved for the rest of her days.

But you said you would help me. You have to help me escape, I said. We can do it together.

We can't, she said. There's no way over the border. There's no escape. I have a visa. Calla. It has to be me.

Take another baby then. Find someone else's. Not mine, I said. Please.

She held out her hands, imploring. We don't have much time.

My stomach swooped, my mouth filled with bile. I could no longer look at Marisol. I need to be alone with her, I said. Marisol nodded, levered herself up from the floor too quickly, so eager, so sure. She opened the door and left the room. I'll wait out here, she said from the other side.

The sound of her body settling down on to the floor. Childless body, still changed. I thought of her as the chimera, of the cells in her bloodstream. And myself as the chimera too. Half animal, half myself. I had been changed irrevocably. I had wanted that. My wanting was no longer important. My wanting could split me apart now and still it would be irrelevant. I thought about a strange woman taking my baby into her home. I thought about Marisol whispering into the ear of Doctor A.

I knew the border was nearby. That was why Marisol had brought us here in the first place. There was a window I could try to force. Or an open door behind me, a corridor to run down. I could get past Marisol, knock the wind from her, but then there would be more people to pass, people with weapons, locked doors, syringes, and I didn't know if I had the strength or cunning to bring us through all that unscathed. I was bleeding still, and slow, the stitches pulling with every step. I cried all over my baby. I thought about the single note of my instinct, how it had got us so far, whether the time had come to go against it, whether that was what it meant to be a good mother after all. To do the right thing when it felt wrong in every bone of your body.

No, I said again, but with less conviction. I leaned my head against the wall. I breathed in the smell of Nova's new body. She started crying, hungry, and I opened the buttons of my dress with movements already instinctive. Marisol came back in and for the first time I noticed damp spots on her T-shirt where the white coat fell open. She saw me looking. Your body does not forget as quickly as you would like, she said. It's the crying that does it.

She knelt down in front of me. If you don't give her to me, they'll take her anyway. Give her to me and she'll never know any of this.

I imagined my daughter grown, a locket around her neck, but only decorative. Only hollow. Nothing inside to tell the world her future, or where she came from. No wilderness to move through. I imagined her among trees, among clean air. I imagined her running very fast, but not away from anything.

Please, Marisol said.

I nodded once, slowly. I handed her over.

Nova opened her mouth and wailed. Her lungs were magnificent. Alarm-pitch cutting through air, proclaiming her alive. That's right, I said to her. You make that noise and you never stop making it your entire life. That's your voice. That's the best thing you have.

Marisol held her awkwardly, seemed surprised at how difficult it was. I had to show her. Like this, I said, positioning Nova against her chest. I did not fall to the floor. I did not crumple.

Find us if you can, Marisol told me, but I knew by her face she thought I would not, that she was going through the motions. She made a move that might have been to kiss me, but thought better of it. Instead she raised a hand in a small, solemn gesture. I understood it as a thank you. I understood it as meaning that we had been through so much together, and that finally it was the end. I watched my daughter disappear, still crying. All that was visible of her was the top of her head, the little shock of dark hair, the edge of the blanket where it rucked up around her face, kept her swaddled and close. Maybe she would not notice me gone until they passed the border. Maybe she would never notice me gone, was too young, too new, flung into the world without ceremony, and maybe it was best that way, whatever I felt, whatever I wanted.

3

I waited in the now-empty nursery for something to happen, but nobody came for me. Eventually I returned to my own room. I sat on the pink bed and wondered if it had been real. Not even a year had passed since that other night in another room when I had pulled wire from my own body. It did not seem strictly possible, but it was the truth. I put my face into my hands, held myself. Somewhere Marisol was holding my baby in the back of a car, getting used to her weight, crossing the glowing line on the ground. Her body was becoming my daughter's comfort. I was left with nothing but my own body, the pain spilling like the milk beading my skin when my arms accidentally brushed against my nipples.

I never saw Doctor A again. In the morning an emissary knocked on my door. She was solemn, respectful. I had passed. Or I was no longer a person of interest. I found that I no longer cared at all. She gave me a change of clothes, a rucksack. In the bathroom I showered and changed and examined what had been given to me. The rucksack did not contain a tent or a map or weapons, only a small soap, a towel, a cereal bar and a bottle of water, and some money in a simple black canvas purse. Outside there was a coach waiting for me, striped with pastel colours along the side. The doors opened with a low hiss. I was alone; I sat at the back, folded up my knees against the seat in front of me, wrote the word

Nova with my finger on the window, so that when condensation flushed the glass her name would be there, waiting. Someone else would sit in this seat and they would see her name and they would know it. I bit my nails down to the skin, wishing my teeth were sharper.

The coach drove down through the country I had crossed so slowly. We stopped periodically for other women to board, women who had the same rucksack as me. We did not speak. We lay our heads against the windows and watched the road move underneath us. No music from the speakers. Rain came in from the slice of open window near the roof.

A few hours passed and we pulled into a service station. The driver took a count as we got off the coach, but nobody was really watching us. We were allowed to go and use the bathroom and buy things. I got myself fries and a pink milkshake and left them untouched on a table, the ice cream congealing at the top.

In the gift shop I bought cigarettes, my old brand, comforting shape in the hand. I went outside to smoke them. Beyond the car park there was a little patch of not-quite woodland, scrubby trees polluted by so many cars, so many coaches, people moving onwards and backwards. I felt all the threads of these lives tangling in mine. I watched a woman with red lips and a red car close her door behind her, near me. She glanced at me and looked away. The early-evening light looked fluorescent behind the service station, radiating gently outwards. The slick of petrol on the tarmac didn't trigger anything in me any more, my senses no longer heightened, no more arcane cravings, no radar. My rucksack was on my back. Nobody was getting back on to the coach yet. I tried the door of the red car, but it didn't open. I turned and walked away from the car park, a little way into the trees. The ground was strewn with cans, scraps of bright plastic, cigarette butts. Beyond the trees there was road. Beyond that road there was green.

I'm coming, I said to nobody. The cars closer, the road leading else-where. The glowing filled me still, reminding me of where I had to go, however long it would take. My body still a reminder. It would never stop reminding me. I'll see you soon, I said.

Epilogue

Sometimes I still think of Marisol swimming from the car she drove into the lake; her body just starting to show but agile in the water, the shape of her silhouetted against the surface as she swam, hard and true. I never saw her like that, but I feel like I did.

I dream of her too. Sometimes in the dream she is my mother, whose face I didn't know. Sometimes in the dream she is dead and sometimes so am I.

In the most frequently recurring dream I am sitting across from her at the table of a roadside diner. She smiles. There is a small cut on her face, near her mouth, almost at the end of healing, but her eyes are bright.

I have somebody I want you to meet, she says.

She lifts Nova over the table to me, like a gift, and I take her without question. It is the only apology I needed or will ever need.

She moves like a thing come from the ground. She moves in the way of ancient and eternal things. I kiss her head. I support her neck, instinctively, even in the dream.

Look, I say to all present. Look who it is.

Acknowledgements

A large portion of a later draft of this book was written during my time as Gladstone's Library Writer in Residence – it would not be what it is without the time, support, resources and research that my month there made possible, and I'm eternally grateful to all of you.

Thank you to my UK agent, friend and forever champion, Harriet Moore, for believing in this book from the first sentences, and to the rest of the team at David Higham – superstars all of you.

Thank you to my US agent, Grainne, and everyone at Fletcher & Co. for looking after my book so well across the pond.

Thank you to my brilliant editors Hermione, Margo and Deborah, who saw this book for what it could be and made it all possible. I'm very grateful to everyone at Hamish Hamilton and Penguin General, Doubleday and Hamish Hamilton Canada.

Thank you to everyone who read *The Water Cure*, and to all the kind strangers I've met since its publication.

Thank you to all the friends and family who gave me encouragement, support, inspiration, beauty, blue talismans and more. You know who you are.

Thank you to everyone who talked honestly with me about motherhood and babies in the last few years — all those who shared their reasons and feelings, gave me hope, scared and reassured me, let me hold their children.

Thank you to Christopher, for everything.